William Patrick Ryan

Literary London

Its Lights and Comedies

William Patrick Ryan

Literary London
Its Lights and Comedies

ISBN/EAN: 9783744768849

Printed in Europe, USA, Canada, Australia, Japan

Cover: Foto ©Andreas Hilbeck / pixelio.de

More available books at **www.hansebooks.com**

"STARLIGHT THROUGH THE THATCH."
A NOVEL.

"The author is an artist. He has made his characters live and speak. He has all the style and polish of an excellent writer.... Quick humour and keen sympathy."

Saturday Review.

"Shows a command of humour and pathos.... A power of original observation and presentment."

The Athenæum.

"'All that is best of dark and bright'.... The story is extremely fascinating."

The Worla.

"Harum-scarum Irish adventure, pathos, and kindliness."

Spectator.

"The pictures have been evidently and faithfully drawn direct from life. An interesting story and a yet more interesting study of ideals and ideas."

Truth.

"The author understands the Irish temperament, appreciates its humour and pathos, and, what is better, knows how to convey that temperament to his readers."

Star.

"A large amount of dramatic incident.... a racy. humorous vein that is thoroughly refreshing."

Catholic Times

LITERARY LONDON
ITS LIGHTS & COMEDIES

BY

W. P. RYAN

Printed by BINGER BROS
110, St. Martin's Lane, London W. C.
at their Works in Amsterdam.

LITERARY LONDON

ITS LIGHTS & COMEDIES

BY

W. P. RYAN

LEONARD SMITHERS

ROYAL ARCADE LONDON W

1898

CONTENTS

THE GREAT YOUNG MAN AND THE NEW STYLE OF LITERARY HISTORY

The great young man is very much with us in "literature" just now. I have tried to keep pace with the sundry manifestations of his intellect, with the things in his person and property which set the admiring crowd of paragraphists about him to prompt and persistent pencilling. In my moments of daring energy I have had thoughts of preparing what I might call "A Small Fry 'Cyclopædia," the full and faithful record of the works, appetites, pastimes, idiosyncrasies, and attitudes of our great young men. These things sprawl across the small-talk journals and are laid as with a trowel on the papers whose *forte* is interviewing. It seems to me that such momentous matters should be reduced to some system, and the wildering wealth of delectable data about our great young men set in handy order for reference by an interested posterity.

We find, for example, that one eminent young man has a keen taste for duck-eggs, that another plays light fantastic tricks with his tooth pick the while he enlightens the interviewer on the progress of the species since he published his "Passion of a Potboiler," in 1896. The inspiration of a third is never really quickened till he has had his morning's dish of mushrooms, and a fourth cannot possibly preserve his standard of realism if peradventure there is an undarned spot in his seagreen stockings. Now, all this will be as intricate as the Catacombs or the labyrinths of Egypt to posterity, if doled out in the haphazard and promiscuous manner we have seen every day. We, who have the privilege of living in an age when our great young men are so graciously communicative, should make some effort to tabulate and systematise their revealings. My projected "Small Fry 'Cyclopædia" would be an effort in this direction.

I must admit, of course that many of the personalities I have in my mind's eye could not be adequately described as Small Fry. We should hunt out, for the purpose of covering them, some medium term. I would not insult them by saying that they are small fry even compared with Shakespeare or Mr. Bernard Shaw. * But the reader will understand the principle I am insisting upon ; the principle that it is a holy and whole-

---

* The man who became a dramatist to amuse himself — on his own showing, — and a demagogue to amuse other people. A great-hearted Celtic sentimentalist who tries to check the overwhelming flow of his sentiment by applications of vegetarianism and cynicism, which superficial observers mistake for his real faith and self. While chastening himself he confuses the issue and the understanding of his contemporaries by a too tantalising desire to chasten other people. He is best known in the rôles of Puck turned Fabian, or Puck turned dramatic critic.

some thought to snap up and enshrine jealously in some permanent form for posterity, the intimate, matutinal, decorative and kindred details of which the younger litterateurs are so generous in our time. Never was there an age when Literature was so communicative ; whether at the supper-table, in the smoking-room, the surgery, the bathroom or the back yard. Too soon if we treasure not these engaging revelations it may grow Shy : for tender is the green plant of its confidence.

For a few years to come I and the labourers like me need not concern ourselves with anything beyond collecting and recording ; systematizing will come later. The plan is simplicity itself. We have only to set the younger school in alphabetical order in our colossal commonplace books, and jot down their little essays about themselves or the character-sketches by their friends from day to day. Let me take a few supreme examples at random :

Morrison (Arthur). A young man of the great Henley School who interviewed a local parson and swept out a reeking little slum for material on which he laboured many days, and evolved a grim though presentable book called "A Child of the Jago." It showed considerable restraint and a very tolerable measure of art, and though adding no vital or finished character to contemporary literature, and giving an erroneous impression of the East End as a whole, was yet a fairly creditable performance. It met many bitter enemies who insisted on regarding it as a contemporary classic, and shouting down and pelting with stones any other would-be pioneer who approached within measurable distance of any slum to the North or South of the Thames. While they stood guard there, Mr. Morrison retired to Loughton where he "stays quietly," delighting in "pottering about," according to his historian, Mr. Clarence Rook, * and collecting Japanese prints. Mr. Rook writes with becoming solemnity about Mr Morrison's "method of work." "He does not sit at a desk, dipping a meditative pen in ink." Oh, no! "He curls himself into the most comfortable chair he can find, and writes with a pencil slowly, steadily, certainly." How the mind is fascinated by that picture of awful resolution, perseverance, fate! It has almost the inevitableness of Greek tragedy! "On the first page of the manuscript there are a few erasures and corrections." God wot!

There is a further story that the wood of the pencil must be of Kentish manufacture, the pointing must have been done by a gold-hafted knife held in the untrembling hand of a golden-haired maiden fed on rose-leaves and love-songs for a twelve-month and a day; and the end must be as fine as one of Mr. Le Gallienne's fancies. This, however, is regarded by some biographers as not absolutely authoritative.

Pemberton (*Max*).   I had scanned some pleasant and eminently readable stories by Mr. Pemberton, but it

---

* In the Chicago *Chap Book*.

was Mr. Coulson Kernahan who first brought me the full vision of his martial and prancing genius. To be sure, it was in the American *Bookman* (May '97) and Mr Kernahan was writing in the language understanded of the American Eagle, laughing in his sleeve no doubt at the open-mouthed wonder with which that easily duped bird took in the whole. Brain-dazzling at any rate was the tale of the right awful extent of Mr. Pemberton's performances. Mr. Pemberton has been "magnificently mendacious" and "mendaciously magnificent." Reading him was "like riding in a hansom cab behind a run-away horse." His stories "left his public agape with imbecile amazement." (How aptly this described the great American public suffering from the Trilby craze!) He rode "abreast with Jules Verne on the high road of fame." Then he "suddenly turned bridle"—clear the way, ye rabble, and God preserve us all!—but, lo! the development was not so desperate as we feared ; we merely heard the clatter of his good steed in the company of Dr. Conan Doyle. No one was hurt.

We hear later (anent a book of a different character) of "the absinthe of pure Pemberton undiluted by facts," but a subsequent cup ("Christine of the Hills") we are now putting to our lips "has been filled from the well of truth." (So that, after many days to reset the old proverb, you can bring the runaway cab-horse to the well, and he can make you drink!) Again we learn that the great charm of the thing is its freshness. Surely, surely! Does Mr Kernahan suppose that water from the well of truth, per the Great Pemberton Water Company, could be other than fresh? Why, in that event, imagine the deputations to the Mr. Chaplin of Literature! * Finally Mr. Kernahan grows sternly critical, and takes Mr. Pemberton to task on more than one point, but altogether—though the metaphors are applied to different books—the cynic might sing the situation thus :

"What's all the bloomin' row about?" said Coulson on parade.
"It's Pemberton broke out again," the colour-sergeant said.
"The 'cab-horse' to the 'well of truth' is bolting, I'm afraid,
"And Jules Verne's green with envy all the morning.

"And Weyman feels a wee man now, and Hope's forlorn and low,
"But Sherlock Doyle from Hindhead hies to see the gallant show.
"The heart wild beats in Levett-Yeats and Haggard's soul's aglow,
"For the 'cab-horse' seems to kick the stars of morning.

"How fares the fiery charger now?" said Coulson on parade,
"Like twenty tartars to a plough!" the colour-sergeant said,
"But gods! he stops! he droops! he drops!—he slumbers in the shade!—
"Someone's read him Miss Corelli in the morning!"

Wells (H. G.). A young novelist and genius of Worcester Park, Surrey. He has brought the microbe, the

---

* Sometimes Sir Walter Besant, sometimes the literary editor of the *Daily Chronicle.*

Martian, and sundry parboiled scientific things into romance. His pleasant, frankly youthful cock-sureness on various occasions indicates that he is of Henleyite training. Rude critics who refuse to take their opinions from Henleyite reviewers insist that he is merely a man of one book. He has hammocks in his garden for interviewers. He likes croquet. He has a "diffident way which is infinitely alarming" * ; he calls his books poor, describes the first things which come into one's mind as "Slush," and with a deprecating wave of the hand insinuates that altogether he has penned no more than a paltry three hundred thousand words,—less, he adds, than one of Dickens' novels. Who could find it in his heart to murmur that, mayhap, in other essentials, too, Dickens' novel has the upper hand? Mr. Wells has a keen taste in churchwardens, and smokes only Martian-cum-Moonshine tobacco (The Bashful Brand) Mr. Wells thinks there is no doubt that the public feels more interested in a man's work if he goes about in, say, a pair of bright scarlet breeches. Mr. Wells has not got quite so far as the scarlet breeches. But he sometimes adopts a Panama Straw Hat. When he dons that Panama Straw Hat (six seven-eighths, or thereabouts) there is something so supremely bland about him that the mere sight of him would soothe and reassure the stricken soul of Mr. L. F. Austin on the historic occasion when he thought Mr. Wells' Martian in-

* Vide *To-Day*.

15

vaders were playing the devil's tattoo on his handle-
bars as he cycled in the dusk through Weybridge. (Any
reader who has forgotten the story may expect to come
up with it again in a new edition of "At Random").

In still more social moments he bends to "Certain
Personal Matters," and a homely beauty wraps him as
he discourses on the domestic coal-scuttle, wife-finding,
and the proper dietary of authors. At such a time one
feels that we require the counterpart of Mr. Yeats' "Shy
One":

> She carries in the dishes
>   And she lays them in a row—
> To an Isle in the Water
>   With her I would go!

We seem to hear the Spirit of Femininity singing:

> He carries in the scuttle
>   And he makes the cinders glow
> While Passion's roaring bellows
>   Within my heart doth blow—
> To red Mars, or any stars,
>   With him I would go!

It were too bad if Mr. Kernahan, able and good-natured, the interpreter of Mr. Pemberton, and the author
of "A Dead Man's Diary," "God and the Ant," "Sorrow
and Song," and other works, should not also have found
his historian. Mr. "Archibald Cromwell" is the man.
One gathers from Mr. "Cromwell" * that Mr. Kerna-

---

* In the *Windsor Magazine*.

16

han is happy as the day is long. He is an optimist and an enthusiast. He has a home by the sea, he thinks birds are praiseworthy poets, and politics a bore. He retains a boyish impulsiveness though he suggests the military man. "His sympathy with the poor and unfortunate is only restricted when organ-grinders are concerned. He walks fast, talks fast, and writes fast, but lives slowly, preferring the serenity of home to ' the hurrying delight' of publicity." He is happy—perhaps—in his historian.

The Kailyarders. Kailyard lore is a very Klondike in itself. You will learn one day how Mr. Crockett uses two specially-constructed £ 100 type-writers (simultaneously?) and talks to a roomful of people the while he writes out his stories. This of course explains at once to many minds certain hitherto inexplicable features of his fiction. Another day as you hear with blank dismay that a body of youthful Scottish writers is meeting in solemn convention in Glasgow, and you shudder at the terrible thought of another relay of Kailyarders, you find the author of "The Raiders" thus addressing the braw laddies :

"Ere long you will be calling 'Fore' to the poor "slow-coaches of professional writers ahead of you, cum-"berers of the green, larry-lag-behinds in the race of "letters. Well, when that comes to pass, we will touch "our caps with what grace we may—and let you pass. "Go on and prosper. I have found no better motto for

"the encouragement of a writer's own heart in his task,
"than the old Aberdonian College one :

> "They say!
> "What say they?
> "Let them say,
> > "Faithfully yours,
> > > S. R. Crockett."

On sober reflection you hope they will hurry up. The change must needs be for the better. You hear the next week or so from Mr. Crockett's own lips that every morning, summer and winter, he has had his cold tub and is ready to begin work by half past four. * At the dawn "everything seems possible" to him, even the writing of Southern English, and at sunrise he "shares in the sense of being newly born." The new-born one can "think better when the birds are getting up than later." "The birds and I are great friends." The simplicity of both parties to the contract is surely on a par. Brought up strictly, Mr. Crockett, dear little soul, was "a lonely child," but he found "vast amusement in telling myself stories." Posterity, the cynics think, may elect that in the matter of an audience his last state shall be worse than his first. "Four miles across the moors I had to walk to school, escorted by a well-beloved dog"—surely a symbol, a foreshadowing of the *British Weekly!*— "and as I journeyed, the stories wove themselves in my

---

* Vide *Black and White*, wherein this and the ensuing confidences of Mr. Crockett appeared.

brain. Then I told them to my school-fellows, and if they refused to laugh at my humour I often fell upon them and smote them." Poor little sufferers, they were no better than the grown generation that succeeded ; but you see that thus early the Kailyard method of extending popularity was in the budding, if not the blowing. Hear Mr. Crockett further:

"*Apropos* of telling stories, I remember once taking "a boy out in a boat with me on the loch, one fearfully "black night, and relating to him a ghastly tale which "I had concocted for the purpose. I worked up a fabric "of horrors, upon which he hung with bated breath, "and eyes starting in the darkness. At the climax I "gave vent to a blood-curdling yell, which completely "upset my audience, and nearly upset the boat, for he "leaped up, and would have fallen into the water had I "not caught him, conscience-stricken in the moment of "my success."

Barring the sensitive conscience, the Crockett method does not seem to have undergone much change since those dear old days.

Ian Maclaren and J. M. Barrie are no match for the great Raider in the art of reading his history in the nation's eyes. They are shy enough to hide behind their books, but the "worth a guinea a box" air hangs about Mr. Crockett like a garment when he walks abroad or unburdens himself at home to the interviewer. Major Pond, Transatlantic lecture agent, whose first subject was Eliza, revolted wife of Brigham Young, and whose eye is unerring for any species of *poseur*, so appreciated Mr. Crockett's pre-eminence in the Kailyard, and the picturesque appeal he makes to the literary gallery generally, that having failed to come to terms with Mr. Hall Caine, he went northwards to St. Andrews, where the great Kailyarder was on golfing bent, and pursued him with his kodak for a full mile of the course. His snapshots must certainly "lick creation" and beat Barnum beyond the Atlantic; which could never be the case were the subjects from plain Barrie or mild Maclaren.

Hocking (Silas), Perhaps the worst thing posterity can say about Mr. Barrie is that he made copy of his mother. For one fearful season we lay in dread that his example was to be copied far and wide—a veritable boom in mothers. Mr. Silas K. Hocking, who would figure considerably in my 'Cyclopædia, was early in the field. Who did not shudder at his ominous declaration in the *Temple Magazine*, after he had enlarged on the greatness of Mr. Barrie's deed, and the prevalence of Margaret Ogilvys in England?—

"I knew one such mother, knew her intimately. Her "face was the first I saw in the morning, the last I saw "at night. Her hands were strong when mine were "weak, and clear her eyes of faith when mine had not "begun to see. Among the nobler mothers of the world "she deserves a foremost place."

We had heard about the men who would peep and botanise upon their mothers' graves. We were not quite sure that their attitude was not preferable to this new extreme of maudlin mammiolatry. However, the day of literary mammiolatry was not to be just yet. Mr. Hocking merely went home to Hampstead and carried on his mild-mannered rivalry with the genius of the Rev. E. P. Roe of America in a novel, "In Spite of Fate," which moved a provincial critic to the rapturous profession of faith: "Should Mr. Hocking write no more, his niche in English literature is now filled." Please, Mr. Hocking, take the critic at his word!

Upward (Allen). Of Mr. Allen Upward I should have myriad things to write in my projected volume. Mr. Upward likes to see life from divergent points. He is a man who can do several things well. In the morning it is almost a toss-up with him whether he shall take to his yacht, fight the Turks, turn out a thousand lines in rhyme, pursue the law, drop into politics, take up history, lift the veil from the secrets of European courts. Yachting, oratory, the law, politics, after-dinner speaking, history, playwriting, are his crack subjects. Now that I think of it, the weaving of fiction must be added to the list. The average man might give this the first or only place, but the average man little knows Mr. Upward. Over his pleasant city chambers he might put the truthful and appropriate announcement: "Dramas, novels, epics, speeches, ghost-stories, and jokes done or repaired while you wait. All orders executed with the utmost neatness and despatch. *Mens Conscia recti.*" He is the promptest, most level-headed, most business-spirited, least inspired man (he laughs at the idea of inspiration) in the whole literary profession.

The Henleyites. The proceedings of Mr. Henley and his "school" would be well within my province, and would affort me some piquant and pleasant diversions. The longer we live the more curious specimens do we chance upon of young men who would fain look immeasurably older than their years, who talk as we might talk of the Elizabethans, of the *National Observer* and the magnificent times when a certain brilliant and burly iconoclast was Cock of the Old Walk. They are sometimes puzzling contradictions. If the Master has taught them any abiding lesson it is surely to break the peace in the literary world on all occasions; yet, they cannot shake away their dallying youth, and they are not always alert to the fact that the England of our time is a supremely different England from what it was up to ten o'clock the morning the "Song of the Sword" was published. They cannot shake off their ingenuous youth and its giddy suggestions, and some few of them cannot overcome an innate taste for the airy-fairy and the daintily bloodless. Hence, in social life, the Panama Straw Hat of Mr. Wells, the Curl-Me-In-My-Chair indulgences of Mr. Morrison, and in the literary world the "Make-Believe" rosewater of Mr. H. D. Lowry. These feather-bed lapses so soon after the Revolution are painfully abnormal, if not positively depressing. There are times when one asks one's self, if, apart from that "Hades of an Epic" smack for Sir Lewis Morris, the *National Observer* may not have gone to press in vain. Yet when all is said and done, the Henley period has left us Mr. Charles

Whibley ("The Yellow Dwarf" *) and the Essay on Burns.

Frederic (Harold). Mr. Harold Frederic, late of Utica, N. Y., now of the National Liberal Club and the *Daily Chronicle*, novelist, reporter, mirror to America of Europe, Asia, Africa and Oceana, biographer of the German Emperor, and expected author of the Complete Index to the Angelic Attributes of Mr. T. M. Healy, would also take a large section of my volume. And these are only a few meagre specimens of the things which would fill my 'Cyclopædia. New parts would be issued weekly or monthly, with ever-new details supplied by the industrious purveyors of Sybil and oracular intelligence, Mr. Clarence Rook, Mr. A. H. Lawrence, and the unconquerable Mrs. Sarah Tooley. And every month—nay, every day,—new worlds of thought and things would be arising on which our lions could declare themselves, open their hearts, and unbosom their souls. We would learn to-day how much Mr. Hall Caine weighed the day he began. "The Christian," and how much he weighed when, with tear-dimmed eye, he wrote "The End," and thanked Heaven ; to-morrow he would be free to tell us whether the daily food of the "Colossal novelist" should contain an undue proportion of starchy or fatty materials. Mr. Shorter might be induced to reveal whether beans or

* Mr. Whibley's association with tho *Yellow Book* links directly of course those supreme outcomes of our dying century, the Henley and Beardsley periods.

23

peas are the more conducive to perseverance on the lines of Brontë research ; Mr. Crockett might describe the sensation of golfing under the Transatlantic snapshot ; Mr. Fred. Whishaw, who, his admirers say, has released us from the painful necessity of depending on a mere Tolstoi or Turgenieff for our impressions of Russia, and who shook his head gravely and told one of Mr. Jerome's young men that trouble between England and the land of the Czar is simply not to be thought of —Mr. Whishaw might unbosom himself on the ideal dietary of a Foreign Minister who wanted to keep in a patient mood with the land of the Steppes. Mr. W. W. Jacobs, the smart young Civil Servant who gives us pleasant bits of fairly interesting barge life in the leisure snatched from St. Martins-le-Grand, and unendurably trite things about humour in general and his childhood in particular through the medium of interviews, would probably oblige us with an occasional bulletin regarding those seven tomatoes and that large cucumber which one of our standard interviewers has assured us form the distinction and delight of the young author's garden.

Truly the possibilities of this ever-growing 'Cyclopædia are entrancing and marvellous.

One or two disappointments for the curious inquirer it were bound to possess. It would know nothing, or next to nothing, of the Dreamer of the Ghetto. Mr. Zangwill stands alone. The spirit of Literature may go to Kilburn, the paragraphist does not. Aloof from the potent cliques and the great coteries, unloved of Fleet

Street, distrusted of Worcester Park, Mr. Zangwill is fain to content himself with the comedies and tragedies of the Ghetto, with looking humanity full in the face, and in the heart, and obstinately going whither his artistic sense may lead him. He is Without Prejudice. But he is a literary wag withal. Haply paragraphic neglect has made him reckless. We all remember the big book he gave us with the title I have just quoted ; a book in which he was not altogether deferential to our great young men. Yet was it a sort of whimsical reflection of himself. Though it left the reader at times with a stunned lost sense, as if he had found himself after many days in an opulent, interminable pantechnicon, yet under the cumbrous burden and the odds and ends piled sky-high, a strenuous, broad shouldered, whimsical, seeing nature ambled along and cared for nobody. Yet was he a poet and a romancist ; pausing awhile as he had a vision of "Eternal Beauty wandering on her way" ; pensive as he detected the thoughts too deep for tears. One felt that by-and-by, when, after these careless, go-as-you-please excursions, he wended him homeward to his study, and the deliberate artistic mood came upon him, he would have the wherewithal to pen lasting things.

Perhaps he may get along after all without the paragraphists. He has never a hammock in his garden at Kilburn should the interviewers grow kindly ; but failing this the fateful question arises : Be there any via media to popularity and posterity ?

I am sorry also to see Mr. Arthur Symons in such

slight favour with the new order of literary historians. In his case, perhaps, his poetry has done something to frighten them. I remember a note in Mr. Mallock's (late) *British Review* to the effect that Mr. Symons reminded the writer of a drunken man whose lips voiced beautiful music. Mr. Symons does not dress up or live up to the ideal either of Mr. Mallock's critic or the Man in the Street. As you meet the young poet, critic, ex-editor of the *Savoy*, in his peaceful haunt in the Temple, you laugh at the absurdity of the Mallock simile. For he is compact of gentleness, culture, and that gracious thing, charm. It seems strangely incongruous that he could think of decadance. Only, if by chance you raise the question, he will give you a forcible and interesting defence of one's right to give any mood or emotion artistic expression. But that is another story. Critical, cultured, poetical, courageous and sensitive to most modern moods, remaining an interesting personality who can do a number of things well, one wonders if he may also realise the hope of the observers who believe that he can do one or two things memorably. Apparently the new style of literary historians will not help him. Fountain Court is as alien to them as Kilburn. It is bad, it is distressing. Yet, remembering also Box Hill and Putney Hill, with the ignored authors of "Richard Feverel" and "Atalanta In Calydon" we take heart of grace after all.

YELLOW MEMORIES—MAX

Old men recall with vivid memory the fierce new intellectual sensation which came with the publication of Swinburne's "Poems and Ballads" or "Songs Before Sunrise." With something of a similar thrill do we of these lonesome latter years re-live that æon of vehement decadence when Mr. Lane and his literary Lilliputians marched across our stage. Æon of Aubrey Beardsley and Sister Egerton and the *Yellow Book!* One looks back to it all in the background of history as to a weird winter when wild and shrieking shapes came down from the desolate hills through the mists, and mocked us through the windows, looking in on our waning study fires, the while unaccountable gray dogs were howling in the distance! O myths, and mists, and marvels of the Beardsley period!

And it came to pass that after many days of Yellow melancholy, the organ of the initiated, the never enough-to-be-immortalised *Yellow Book* sowed its wild oats as it were and took a villa in Streatham. Or we might change the metaphor and say that it was no longer a

27

lurid comet of literature; it walked on the plain earth
sedately and soberly; moving no more to the music of
"key-note" or she-note, looking neither to the right
where Miss Modernity flaunted her flag nor to the left
where Mr. Aubrey Beardsley groped through gaunt
plantasies suggestive sometimes of an artistic Don
Quixote waking up from a night-mare wherein he had
tilted at innumerable weird windmills. It had grown
serious and respectable, and—it had taken to Literature! Lovers of the abnormal were sad. "There was
nothing like it," they said, "in the dear, fantastic, ut-
terly-utter stage that is now no more." They prophe-
sied poor times—the deepest of "slumps"—for it, believ-
ing that respectability could never prosper. And gradually the music of "key-note" and she-note grew subdued, its heart failed it, and the foe called it ordinary
as old boots. The Philistine dubbed it "a yellow halo
hovering round decay."

* *
*

In November '97 we learned at long last that its
career as an illustrated quarterly was over, that if it ever
appeared again, the nature and system of the literary
contents would not be as of old. The announcement
marked the last dripping drop of a spent literary current which had theatened once upon a time to become
a very deluge. Then indeed could the world say that
the Beardsley period was at rest for ever. Yet haply
not at rest. Perchance it still groans uneasily and paws
the air of eternal night with long, lean, tortuous hands

in the might-mare limbo to which time has consigned it.
Alack! Alack!

* *
*

Max Beerbohm is the most interesting survival—
the Survival of the Fittest—from the Beardsley period.
Cynics indeed are wont to trace him with some semblance of reason to a yet earlier one! Max was born
on August 24th, 1872. Curiously enough, it is not on
record that there were any special portents in the heavens that year. The solar system gave no extra thrill.
Comets were not about, and seers have left no stories
of alarming and inexplicable visions. But after all,
destiny and the gods are calm ; it is man, mere man,
who makes a pother o'er his triumphs. Nature could
afford to hold her peace about one of her masterpieces.
So there were no unusual signs and wonders in the land
that fateful August, 1872. Yes, there was one. There
was the baby Beardsley. Mr. John Lane, the biblio-
grapher of Max, (his minor rôle is publishing) has
searched the files of the *Times* in our own decade.
Lo! he found that on the day Master Max was born
there had appeared in its columns the following announcement :

"On Wednesday, the 21st August, at Brighton, the
wife of V. P. Beardsley, Esq., of a son."

The antiquaries had stupidly ignored the fact that
the same week saw the entrance into our mundane
sphere of two such reformers as Aubrey Beardsley and
Max Beerbohm! From 1872 to 1894, when the latter

29

found his pride of place in the *Yellow Book*, there is little to be said about the world, except that it witnessed the education of Master Max at Charterhouse, where he is still remembered for his Latin verses, and at Merton, where he matriculated in 1890. He did not devote all his time to educational tedium, for he began the revolutionising of modern literature by contributions to the *Clown*.

The publication of his "Works" differentiated the year 1896 from others since the glacial period or thereabouts. Funny people said the book was hopelessly "young," that the author was a pleasant fop, a cultured dandy, with the semblance of a child's artlessness. Others hinted that he had sold his soul to the polite follies, that his intellectual pose was unutterably languid, that he looked at life with a simper, that he sniffed very gracefully. Yet to say that the time was coarse and his nose was dainty is almost to sum up the 19th century. And what delectable truths he taught us in his grave old infantile way! How smartly he has cut the faddish face of his Age with the little green twig of his satire! How blithe he has been on "Dandies and Dandies," how neat on the expressiveness of dandiacal costume! How Mr. Hall Caine must have opened his deep Manx eyes on learning that seeing him was reading his soul, that his flowing, formless cloak is like one of his own novels, twenty-five editions latent in the folds of it, that melodrama crouches on the brim of his sombrero, that his tie is a Publisher's Announcement, his boots are copyright, that in his bands he holds the staff of the *Family Herald.* As for Mr. Clement Scott— poor inclemently treated Clement of a later phase—of his *Saturday Review* period—well, he may simply be remembered in history as Max's principal butt!

Yet consider how much of our latter day literary life is bound up with those twin towers of sentiment, Mr. Caine and Mr. Clement Scott. Nor Bovril nor the best advertised brand of Cocoa has had more influence in the shaping of modern England. Our infant seer's out-look would have been practically catholic had he also sighted Mr. George R. Sims. Man of the Bull Dogs, Man of the Trotting Ponies ; of the Liver ; the Hair Restorer ; the good old Adelphi Drama, the Lights of Home, Mary Jane's Loves, and "Christmas Day in the Workhouse." Homer of the Whitechapel Road and Shakespeare of the Slums! You never entirely realize the appalling pity which underlies the East End till you come to grasp the fact that to its poorer hundreds of thousands, the knowledge of the graces of literature, of "sweetness and light," and the music of the spheres comes faint and filtered through the ballads of Dago-net!

Passing to the general age, the seeing eye of Max was not impressed. He warned us that we were living a decadent life, nothing but feebleness in us. "We have our societies for the prevention of this and the pro-motion of that, and the propagation of the other, because there are no individuals left among us. Our sexes are nearly assimilate... We are born into a poor weak age. We are not strong enough to be wicked, and the Non-conformist Conscience makes cowards of us all."

His worst enemies admit that the elaborate artificiality of Master Beerbohm's intellectual get-up is interesting, that even his foolish things he says well. In truth a cynical seer and polished Punch, he is a pleasant institution even when the things and atmosphere of the Beardsley period, which explain and in some degree excuse him, have passed away. There is a classic touch in his foppery. He can be a refined, sly-lisping Apamantus. Quaint are his modicums of wit when he waits for inspiration. I recant the opinion I expressed when I was a younger and I fear less balanced critic. "His real hope lies in being a man, absurd though the suggestion seems. Some great influence may yet take him by the ears, and shake a man out of the ridiculous make-up and tout ensemble of his artificiality." No, I believe now that his cap and bells are his *raison d'être.* Judging by some of his latter-day utterances, to be sure I should say that the cap needs a little brushing, the bells just a little tuning. But these are slight details. Let Polite Folly still wrap him round, saying with all the fervour of Titania to Bottom :

> So doth the woodbine the sweet honeysuckle
> Gently entwist; the female ivy so
> Enrings the barky fingers of the elm.
> O, how I love thee, how I dote on thee!

THE DEVIL AND A MODERN
KNIGHT ERRANT

Once on a time the most fiery entity in the literary life of London was the poet-playwright-controversionalist, Lithobolia * Buchanan, who never lost an opportunity of proclaiming that "Nowadays in Hell and London, Truth methinks is sorely needed." He scattered the Truth periodically in showers of large live coals over the latter city, coals so very "live" indeed that one might be pardoned for supposing they had just been doing duty in the other region. He proclaimed from the housetops how much he "loathed the foul materialistic serpent that surrounds the world." In earlier years most judicious critics will admit that he displayed a fair spiritual equipment. The divinity that shapes our ends had found full often his ardent poetical worship. But his spirituality had passed through strange traits. It fought and almost shattered itself against a host of sturdy and distorting things. A fine mind seemed to become warped, to flame with stark unreason, though displaying at times a brave sense of human pity and

---

* *Lithobolia*, the stone-throwing spirit.

33

3

brotherly zeal. He lashed those who failed to accept his guidance, to worship as he worshipped ; to timid Christians he became the embodiment of a new and collossal intellectual Inquisition.

Then apparently he cooled and quietened. The fiery furnace of his controversial nature never attained white heat. He started a book-shop in Soho, and something of the stolidity that doth hedge a shopkeeper brought its distressing sense and heaviness on even him. Had he been a Greek, he would probably like Empedocles have leaped into a volcano ; being a Scotchman, on failing in the fight with his age, he opened a shop. He grew local and damped with the wistfulness of Suburbia, if still unafraid. And mark you, a smouldering volcano in a drab municipality is a sad sight ; sad as an old war-horse yoked to a milk-cart. We associate it to the end with Ætna and Empire, with heighth and width and glory ; it pains us to behold it parochial. It is as if the *Daily Chronicle* were to sink into weary old age as the *Clerkenwell News* again, with Mr. Massingham pleading pathetically for the reform of local sewers, and Mr. Norman confining his international energies to audiences with local lamp-lighters, to say nothing of canvassing for small advertisements in his spare time or doing turns at the "case."

The settling down of our poet-playwright-controversialist was nevertheless a sore puzzle to certain minds of our literary London. Perhaps to those minds the following plain, unvarnished chronicle may afford some assistance in their difficulty. It concerns the year while our friend was still a man of terrible and persistent dogmatism, still laying down the law in thunder to his age, still cursing it and consigning it to many unprofitable and unpleasant places. The words "Superstition," "Shibboleth," "Humbug," were still burning on his lips. He railed at the Average Man and the very hint of a Common or Received Opinion was gall to him.

Lithobolia one unlucky day filled his head with the thought that the Devil was a fine fellow. He forthwith started a fierce propaganda whose aim was to give the Devil his due. He was convinced that the Devil had been maligned from the earliest ages, but that still— gallant gentleman that he was—he persisted, in season and out of season, slander, libel, and contumely notwithstanding, in trying to help and comfort man in man's own despite. The Devil, not the Dog, was the Friend of Man. To be sure some mean critics said that his Devil was a mere bogey man. He was glibly eloquent and vaporous they added. As he talked, spectres fashioned of London fog sat in judgment, as it were, on the majestic star-spheres. The village idiot playing emperor was indeed a sight no more ridiculous than the new Satan on himself. But Lithobolia was true to his Devil.

The misunderstanding began long ago in the Garden of Eden, said Lithobolia. The Devil was really a vegetarian, and vegetarianism and its joys and beauties he sought to preach to Mother Eve. The episode of the forbidden fruit was merely his first practical lesson to her in the ways of honest, go-ahead vegetarianism. Had Eve and Adam been true to his teaching, had they followed up his vegetarian advising, had the world followed in their wake, the human race had grown up sane, strong and conquering, instead of developing into the mean, shrunken, shrivelled, neurotic and idiotic exhibition which we found it. "But I and the Devil will cure it," he cried, as he clenched his fists.

For their own vile purposes the early anti-vegetarians, he went on to say, had deliberately and of malice aforethought misrepresented the Devil's action in the Garden of Eden. They obscured the question by the introduction of a number of nonsensical and irrelevant side issues. Furthermore, quoth he, they piled up fearsome traditions about the Devil's excursions earthward, and about the internal affairs of his far-off dominions. They pictured a hell of fire and brimstone where legion wretches writhed and gasped through all the ages. Even John Milton, sane and sturdy in some things, was no better than the common man in certain of his pictures of the place of penal fire.

"Penal fires indeed!" said Lithobolia scornfully. "Half of hell—or what you call hell—is a delightful place where good vegetarians go when they die, where they feed everlastingly on immortal cabbages, on sacred cauliflowers, on transcending mushrooms, on indescribable Scotch Kail. The other half of hell is simply the scene where these entrancing things are cooked and I admit, of course, that in such a quarter there is a good deal of smoke and flame. The fires are made from all sorts of ugly materials—from damned and unrighteous publishers, from reviewers for the evening papers, from dramatic critics of the Ibsen cult!"

"Yes," continued Lithobolia, as he harangued the multitude, "such is hell; a fair and joyous place. I would go there.—"

And presently there was a wild cry of "Pity you don't!"

"I cannot yet retire to such comfortable quarters," he rejoined, "I have to remain here and make the worth and ways of the Devil clear. I have to bring back this benighted age to a true love for the Devil and vegetarianism."

He went forth with many pamphlets on the Devil's behalf, printed and published at his own expense, and advocating his pet theory in words of flaming passion and noble wrath. "The Devil's Due Library," which he promptly issued, divided the world into two irreconcilable camps. People spoke of the "New Reformation," Lithobolia's "Moral Renaissance," "The Great Human Devil-Cure," and such delectable things. The earth for decades after was a place of intellectual tornadoes.

At last Lithobolia took the notion to drop down to the Devil's own world and see how the agitation was affecting parties there.

To his amazement, when he came to the door of the nether world he found an ominous calm over everything. Charred pillars, blackened ruins, smoke-coloured fragments of dismal walls and halls met his gaze on every hand. But no devil of any sort or shape was apparent. Lithobolia was befogged.

Presently an impish-looking youth ambled up. He chuckled when he saw the visitor.

"Hello!" said the imp, "come down at last! Didn't you hear that hell's been burned out?"

"Go along," said Lithobolia, but his tone had lost its earthly ring and positiveness.

"Fact!" said the imp. "Of course when you began to write in defence of the Devil, we sent the tip to our London agent who bought up for us every spare copy of the book—that explains the tremendous sale, you know. We thought we'd have pleasant afternoon readings."

"And then?"

"The volumes were so fiery, so full of heat, that when we got them in here, what with the other flames, what with —"

"Go on," said Lithobolia, impatiently.

"They took fire, they blazed, and blazed, and blazed, till they burnt the bally place out, devils and all."

"And how did you escape?"

"Oh, I had been a printer's devil in the office where some of your controversial works were set up. I could stand anything. Besides I'd been a salamander in a previous life."

Then a great darkness fell. When Lithobolia groped out of it he found himself on earth. He rubbed his eyes. "Was it a dream?" said he.

Never again was he his old fiery self.

Indeed when he wrote his religious novel, "The Rev. Annabel Lee," he startled the world by ignoring his own brave, independent publishing business in Soho and going back to the ordinary publishing sphere and channels. Mr. Pearson found grace in his eyes! Happy was Lithobolia in the land of the Philistines! Fraternise would he in soft-eyed fondness with those who trim "The rush-lights of Clapham!" Thus comes it to pass as the Prophet foretold, that the cow and the bear now feed, and their young ones lie down together.

Of his subsequent career there is nothing to be said, except that his "Ballad of Mary the Mother" increased our pity for him.

A LUNAR ELOPEMENT:
THE KEY TO ALLEN GAUNT'S
DEFECTION

A joy has gone out of life—let me hope only temporarily. The Women Who etc. play fantastic tricks before high literature no more. The wise grave man who left the realms of science to make revolting petticoats articulate gives no sign in secluded Haslemere that he is true to the mad, bad revolutionary faith of the mid-nineties—Good heavens! how distant the period seems! When he speaks he only adds insult to injury by offering us—guide-books to the Continent! * Guide-books to mere mundane places when the Emancipated Skirt and the Palpitating Petticoat would fain be shown the way to new wonderlands of Did and Didn't!

Even Mr. Hardy has not kept the new faith. We have been pained by the recent intelligence that, wearied of a public which misunderstood his late phase, he was going back disappointed and chastened in spirit to

---

* For the volume on "The Evolution of the Idea of God," his labours began years ago.

the fiction of his earlier manner. Tess and Jude are to be buried so to speak Under the (New) Greenwood Tree. By the way, in the summer of the year of grace '97, he rested for a period by the lake of Geneva. One wonders if "clear, placid Leman" had had anything to do with his decision. We all know how it made passion-tossed Byron wish to exchange "earth's troubled waters" for a "purer spring."

In the pure, placid lakelet of Leman
    Peers Thomas who told us of Tess;
What sees he down deep? Is't the demon
    Of Damseldom's doom and distress?
Hush! he cries: "Silky sins of the sexes—
    O Problem quaint Wessex thought queer—
O View that grim Grundy's soul vexes—
    I bury ye here.

"O pure, placid lakelet of Leman,
    O contrast to Jude and his Jills!
When I gaze to be goody as Weyman
    Is the Hope that my hardened soul fills.
Though for Woman's New Wails I've wept
        oceans
    I bid ye good-bye for ye vex:
Madding Crowd of the maudlin emotions,
    O sweet, sinning Sex!"

Some there be who will tell us that they knew Mr. Hardy to be merely a temporary convert. But they expected permanent faith and unceasing activity from the Great Heart of Haslemere. What has dimmed his light and depressed his enthusiasm? I do not profess to know the whole secret, but let me unfold to you the inner significance of the tragedy of the last book he penned for the Cause. Here it is in his own fashion :

BRITISH BARBARA

My name is Allen Gaunt, and all men ought to know by this time that I have a mission to my age. What I shall do or say next no man knows—not even myself ; but of this you may be sure, that even in fiction I shall say nothing contrary to my own profound beliefs. You may also rest assured that whatever I say will deal directly or indirectly with the marriage question (Alas! the assurance has not been justified), as I long since patented my right, my exclusive right, to the making of sensational discoveries anent that no longer delicate topic. I have had sometimes to abstain from saying many things I did think ; when I wished to purvey strong meat for men, I was compelled to provide a very inferior article for folk that were not men. But in the Polar Star series, to be published at the Ungodly Head, Fie-Go Street, I shall change all that. This is the first story of the series, and deals with my own affairs. In further books I shall be still more at home, for therein I shall deal with the affairs of other people. This is my preface.

Now let me tell you in my usual blunt way about myself and British Barbara.

Barbara was the only one who really saw the full point and significance of my last great work, "The

Woman Who Chid." It came under Barbara's notice in a singular way. She was employed as an assistant by an old woman who kept a sweet-stuff shop in Camberwell, and for wrapping purposes her mistress had bought several copies from a waste-paper dealer. Barbara had been an assiduous reader of halfpenny novelettes, and she was first attracted to the "The Woman Who Chid" by its remarkable similarity in style to her favourites. She read it and was charmed. Next day she sought me out, came into my study unannounced, just as I was cudgelling my brain for a sensational new idea about womankind. She flung herself into my arms and said, "Love, I come to you from the depths of Camberwell. Often therein I have sighed for my soul's mate, and lo! I have found him in you. I am the embodiment of 'The Woman Who Chid.' "

I liked the impulsiveness, the candour, the unconventionality of the dear girl. I thought that I had not lived in vain, for, wonder of wonders, had not my teachings borne fruit in Camberwell?

I said dreamily and fondly, "I am yours, pretty bird." This was our nuptial ceremony.

Then came the supreme question. Where was the spot, the charmed corner of earth, whereon we could lead our truest lives? A vast deal depended on our decision; all the elect would look to us for light and leading. It behoved us to do something ultra-extraordinary. I own I couldn't satisfactorily settle the matter, for novel-writing had begun to tell on my once inventive brain. But Barbara was equal to the occasion.

"Dear," she said, "the solution is very simple. For us the highest altitude of earth is the only possible station. I believe that Mount Everest, of the Himalaya Range, is the highest point in the known world. There we must go. The spot, I understand, is sacred to Theosophic associations. Our home will be on its veriest pinnacle. There, darling, you will write your great novels; and while you wrestle with your superfine problems the mountain goats will be my playmates."

"Done," I said delightedly.

I need not go into the details of our voyage to the East and the first novel month we had on the apex of Everest. I must hurry on to the crowning tragedy.

After a month my own Barbara grew cold to me. It was not easy to be warm on the top of Everest under the best of circumstances, but so far the heat of our matrimonial discussions had kept things pretty hot. Now, however, Barbara never heeded me whatever I said. I grew alarmed: I could not write a word; I began to fear I would soon be forgotten.

One night on coming out of my tent on Everest's top, I heard a pair of most loving voices in converse. My heart almost ceased to beat when I detected the familiar notes of my Barbara. The other actor in the little drama was—now, you'd never guess. It was the moon, the sly sober moon! How the pair blushed when they saw me! The moon said a confused Good-night, and hurried skyward. I caught Barbara by the shoulder and shook her.

"Hands off!" she cried. "Whatever are you a-doin'

44

of? Don't you know that the moon is a respectable woman. Besides, she's my nearest neighbour now, and I must be civil to her."

I was staggered. Certainly the moon was always regarded as a well-behaved female. I had wronged my dear one, though I can't say I ever cared greatly for respectable females, as my stories show plainly enough.

Still, her trysts with the moon became far too many for my taste or my peace. At last I determined to have competent opinion on the subject. I went down into Tibet and consulted the head Mahatma. I found him a little moody, for business was dull with him. Even his correspondence with Mrs. Besant was now a very irregular affair; and the defection of Herbert Burrows and others he described as "a fair knockout."

"Yâ!" he said, when he heard my story. "The moon a female indeed! That fiction has been of life-long use to the same moon, for it has prevented the suspicions of many a wronged husband, I can tell you. The moon is a sly old dodger, and I'd advise you to keep an eye on him."

I hurried home. It was late when I arrived. There wasn't a sign of the moon in the sky. No wonder. When I got to my tent there he was, repeating to Barbara a lot of the amatory sonnet stuff that old poets had addressed to himself under the delusion that he was what he wasn't.

Wild with rage, I took up the MS. of my latest novel, and hurled it full in his face. But the nimble old dog dodged it. Then he shot one of his wicked beams at me. Moonstruck, I fell helplessly under the table.

I crawled to my feet, as he scampered off with Barbara. "I suppose," I cried, "you'll say you're off to the twenty-sixth century."

"No," he laughed, "We're only going for a holiday to St. Tibbs' Eve." And then he kissed Barbara—and shot another beam at me.

And, doubly moonstruck, you can imagine my misery in the world.

Once in the summer of a later year, the Great Heart reappeared for a moment in what we may call that delectable little country pleasure garden so jealously and daintily preserved from the vulgar, and let out to the would-be-considered true and trusty worshippers of Omar Khayyam. There they retire once a year and affect to bring the spirit and atmosphere of the serene, pleasure-loving Persian philosopher to one patch at least of England's conventional soil. It was there our author paid tribute to the Master with an assumed abandon meant to convey the assurance that he was as delightfully "revolted" as ever. He sang:

"No saint—and no sot—was our Omar, I wis,
    But a singer, serene, philosophic;
For Philosophy mellows her mouth to a kiss
    With each step that she takes toward the tropic.
Pale gold is the grain in the vats of the north;
    Lush purple thy grape, Algeciras;
And the creed that is cold by the mists of the Forth
    Glows pink in the gardens of Shiraz."

46

But like all English Omar Khayyamism, it was easy make-believe. L. F. Austin, Henry Norman, and the rest of them must have felt that it was as hollow in reality as their own. Fancy those eminently respectable gentlemen translating the Master's ethics into their lives! Why, they would tremble from their top hats to their patent leather boots at the sight of the singing girl. Even Mr. Norman's imperialism is not wide enough to take in all the Persian spirit. Omar worship is delightful, naïve, a sweet butterfly-chase in an idle hour and a summer field; but as deep as a lady's taste for some shade of chiffon, as permanent as the passion for perfumed baths!

Apropos of Omar, and Mr. Le Gallienne's paraphrase toying with the Persian spirit (we might say that here it suggested a saucy maiden trying in her sweet girlish devilry to preach piquant immoralities to her maiden aunt, and there it set the old Persian pagan to nice music, made his worldly-wisdom dainty, and gave us the occasional impression that he was out sunning himself in a prettily-frilled cycling costume), our hero distinguished himself by one or two bursts of vehement championship of his young poet-friend, whom with brothers Watson and Davidson he grouped apart and crowned as the three living poets of the first order. No wonder that we find in journals of the period the delectable intelligence that somewhere or other Professor Allen Gaunt's Great Literary Show has arrived : that the Professor will compass the most wonderful illusion within the provence of mortal man : he will look like

47

a Critic!—that there's a Marvellous Transformation Scene: where the Tiny Heliconian Triplets, Watson, Le Gallienne, Davidson, after one pat of his hand on each head, will stand forth Poets of the First Order! Finally, we read that in reponse to the usual encore, the Professor will revive his famous old piece of spectacular splendour: The Modern Amazon jumping through a Wedding Ring! Well might those old announcements finish: Walk in, gentlemen, walk in!

THE FLIGHT FROM THE CAINEYARD

"Better be a coward for five minutes, than be dead all the rest of your life," said a witness during the course of the Parnell Commission. Some such thought ran through my own mind on the morning of the 9th of August, 1897 ; but in order to preserve my life I meant to be a coward for at least a fortnight. I am writing for a generation on whose brain the 9th of August 1897 is branded as it were in letters of blood and fire, and ill it would become me to do more than glance in passing at the momentous nature of that date in human annals ; yet I cannot help wondering if posterity in or about A. D. 2097 will realise the emotion which passed through England that never-to-be-forgotten day when Mf. Heinemann launched his five times ten thousand copies of Hall Caine's "Christian" upon the world ; when all London was the Caineyard for the nonce, and a thrill which might be felt passed through this age-old earth from the top of her snow-white Himalayan cap to the innermost point of her axis.

I at least was a coward for the time. In hot haste I arranged to fly from the Caineyard. It is my daily duty in a certain haunt not a thousand miles from Fleet Street to guide or help literary opinion in a small way ; but that morning of mornings I had vanished from the post of duty and, in Stevensonian phrase, "the bright face of danger." My office confrères entirely failed to understand during that first week in August why I made so sudden a decision to finish work for the nonce and prepare for a spell of holiday-taking from the Saturday which was the 7th of the month. When I said, in sundry sudden fits of exultation, and sundry sudden fits of what seemed maliciousness, "I shall be in North Devon on Monday," they were sorely puzzled, and finally, I believe, began to doubt my sanity. Yet it was all a] deep laid scheme ; it was all of malice aforethought. Just as Mr. Heinemann was sending out those 50,000 copies, I was speeding in a South-Western train towards the peaceful dells, the insinuating lanes, and the shy, elusive runlets of North Devon, leaving my literary comrades to their fate.

And lo! to this day I am peacefully ignorant of "the unheard-of business in London," that famous, long-waited-for Monday morning. Nothing troubled me personally beyond a slight crush at Waterloo. I know not how the trumpets sounded and resounded in the Caine-yard. To save my life I could not say if Mr. Heinemann ate an extra rasher for breakfast in honour of the mighty event ; I am ignorant as to the number of Manx cats which on the tiles of Greeba Castle the previous midnight joined in a wild glee-chorus: "Now we shan't be long!" It has not been even revealed to me if the

Daily News critic wrote "Thank God!" at the end of his review. When Caine booms are abroad, whom the Gods love have their holidays. Thus may life be tolerable, though the male Corelli takes the floor!

At Barnstaple I left the border-line of sophisticated civilization, and as I caught the coach for Lynton and its fair sister Lynmouth, I knew that unless fate played me some nasty trick I had really escaped the deep-mouthed heavy bay of the Caineyard blood hounds. The metaphor perhaps needs some excusing, but my imagination was in an excited state that day. I thought, as I sat me on the box seat, and the conductor's bugle mimicked, as it were, what was going on in distant London, how vain is the effort to bar the path of the truly "colossal" novelist. It was hardly three years since I had imagined that Professor Saintsbury had crushed Mr. Hall Caine for ever by the declaration that he was scarcely the equal of Mrs. Radcliffe ; that he had just managed to hit the prevailing sentiment of his time—with all its "vague compound of imperfectly digested philosophical and ethical theory with cheap altruistic sympathies." He belonged to a school which "almost always rants," said the professor in final callousness. The coach-wheels which now dragged heavily up a steep hill-road of Devonshire seemed to grate "Caine! Caine! Caine!" as if in mockery of that tart declaration, and a train bearing down the Great Western line seemed to roar with the voice and volume of the "boom" in the London it had left four or five hours before.

51

Now, the gods are in exile, the dryads, the graces, and even the fairies are gone or going, but we have still to thank the fates that leave us a goodly share of coaching in the West and South-West. (Alas! even here the trail of the light railway is already being laid.) That long afternoon drive with genial Devonians, up hill and down dale, had an old-world sense and charm. The latter part of the journey—through the Lyn valley, by sheer hills crowned with luxuriant greenery, with the river singing, but often hid, in the foliage below—was a veritable charm. It was twilight as we braved the last big hill at Lynton—which John Ridd, you will remember, was anxious to escape when he took his uncle to the Doone valley—and it was deep dusk before I was able to take a stroll round Lynton itself and on to the sea. By that time everyone seemed abed, or, at least, they were not abroad, and Lynton's streets—such as they were— apparently led nowhere. The exhausted earth had gone early to rest after the strain of the fifty thousand copies of "The Christian."

I was puzzled. I had been positively assured that two towns, called Lynton and Lynmouth, lay somewhere thereabouts. Indeed I had actually come upon bits of them myself. I pursued a dim-lighted, lonely patch of street up a hill, and forward saw a house or two at the end of a pleasant path leading seaward. On another hill, a white house—it was really an hotel—stood out from the foliage and seemed to touch the clouds. I followed the intricate, winding lanes along cliff and hillside, but seemed as far as ever from the ocean, whose genial voice I heard below. In the dusk-light, tempered by a modest, ghostly gas-lamp, I got the sense of a lovely, unspoiled, deserted place, touched to life—on high Lynton at least—by a bracing breeze, not so shrill, indeed, but quite as pleasant as the coach-driver's bugle. But by what irony was this named a hoiday resort? I recalled Keats's picture of the place where "sat grey-haired Saturn, quiet as a stone." Like the character in Tennyson.

> "I seemed to move in old memorial tilts,
> And doing battle with forgotten ghosts,
> To dream myself the shadow of a dream."

Often I looked towards the sky that baffling night and asked myself if in sober verity the Caineyard it-self might be no more than "such stuff as dreams are made of."

In the morning I really discovered Lynton, and go-ing downward by zigzag, leafy laneways glistening af-ter a matin shower—as yet I scorned the cliff railway—I also discovered Lynmouth and the shining sea, spread-ing its gallant breast to the mellowed coastline of Wales. My first thought was that it was all good for the con-templative spirit; that if the hermits of old desired any-thing more solemn one must marvel what manner of men they could be. As for either town—or overgrown village—of itself it is unimportant. But the hills, the cliffs, the trees, the greenery, the rocks, the Lyn river, the glens, the lanes winding here, there, and every--where, the views of the sea from so many lovely points high and low, the quaint, zigzag street-lines—truly they made a provincial Elysium. Lynmouth was the first seaside spot that kept my interest alive and had not shown all its sights in twenty-four hours. The solitude was remarkable. Lynmouth, with its sleepy charm, making one eventually almost an æsthetic Rip Van Winkle, was that first day occupied chiefly by myself and copies of "Lorna Doone." And "The Christian" was known of no man!

Myself and Mr. Blackmore's novels continued to be the chief inhabitants of Lynmouth during the succeeding days of my stay. It is a marvel to me that the poets and other ostensible devotees of solitude have not made a hermitage of Lynmouth. They could burrow out delightful little cells in the hills on either side of the bay—if I may call it a bay—or a little interlacing of the branches and shrubs on the great and lonely sides of the Lyn glen should make them ideal "houses." A little fishing daily in the Lyn itself, from the town towards Watersmeet or the Doone valley, would easily supply them with the necessaries of life—unless they have grown luxurious in their tastes. If so, a little Devonshire cream or honey, to be had for little or nothing in any quiet neighbouring restaurant, should not only satisfy, but carry them back in thought to the ambrosial days of the gods upon high Olympus.

In wilder moods they might saunter round the North Walk, running sheer above the sea, to the famous Valley of Rocks, with the Devil's Cheese-knife and the sundry things that shadowed the imagination of the plain yet fanciful John Ridd during that visit to the wise, if vehement, Mother Meldrum. Talking of poets, we know that Coleridge and Wordsworth used to refresh the inner man at an inn in Lynmouth. With that knowledge I really begin to understand some of the languid, ineffective moods of Coleridge. The hills by Lynmouth draw round one subtly, instilling into one's spirit an unearthly restfulness. After a few hours by its waters I had a vague sense of having dozed there in dreamy unconcern for half a century. When that feeling grew pronounced, I took the precaution of ascending either by the cliff railway—which recalls Sir George Newnes—or the ever-fascinating laneways to Lynton on the height. The breeze there was generally sufficient to rouse me to a sense of my past life and my distant relations. Still, as the hours grew, or idly dreamed away, I could not get rid of the feeling that I was rapidly becoming Lynmouth's Oldest Inhabitant. Unconsciously I assumed a paternal air towards everything.

I have mentioned that, apart from myself, the chief inhabitants of Lynmouth were copies of "Lorna Doone." The overpopulation in that respect would have scandalized Malthus. In one shop-window I counted sixteen copies, while bundles lay by the door, on trunks, on counters, under chairs, in soap-boxes, and among odds and ends of crockery. "Lorna Doone" seemed equally at home amid fishing-tackle, fish, fruit, photographs, flowers, ironmongery, and beans. I never saw anyone buy a copy of it in all North Devon—I suppose everybody had read it a dozen times— but everyone seemed to deem it a duty to give the great local classic a generous show. It is supposed to be as good as clotted cream almost to a Devonian. It is certainly a good deal more in evidence in North Devon. I wonder if even Hall himself is similarly close to the heart of the little Manx nation.

I took the classic with me in my various tours from Lynmouth to the choicest spots of the "Lorna Doone" country. It was borne in upon me more and more that John Ridd's story was as closely in touch with the spirit of Devon as was John's simple nature with the still life of his home region. There is a growing pleasure as we see unfolded his close intimacy with the most retiring and unconsidered things of the abundant natural world about him. He will talk of a little runnel with more reverence than might a young knight of old of his ladye. The secrets of moss and tiny blades of grass and elusive streamlets—many Devonshire streamlets may be called elusive—he seems to know. His progress with his story is leisurely indeed—more leisurely than that of the patient ass of his county—but I judge that this leisurely way is characteristic of his people. Among those up-and-down dales, over the cliffs and hills, and by the luxuriant, much-appealing foliage of this fairest of shires, it is hard to picture swift movement as normal or probable. Glen and crag, foliage and watermeet, lay gentle hands on one, detaining one in spite of one's self. Humour here would be out of place in any pronounced or hilarious form; but we can see a natural fitness in the subdued variety of the article offered by John Ridd. We cannot be so patient when his extreme naturalness degenerates once in a while into slight coarseness. But Nature, may-hap, in her most beautiful and bountiful manifestations, cannot preserve us from some betrayals of animalism.

Yes, now and then I shook off the sleepy balm of Lynmouth—lovely, lonely, zigzag, unpretending Lynmouth—and trod the hills, the by-paths, the loitering glens, the "brambly wildernesses" to fair spots of John Ridd's regions. I think I liked the long, devious Lyn glen the best, with its singing river wooed and guarded by unstinted greenery, and the sheer hills on either hand, shutting out man's sounding cities and the things that live a day. Nature is sacramental here—the great Mother Confessor that heareth many confessions. Those charming hills struck the lonely spectator below with some sense of their being, in sooth, "the army of unalterable law," even as (in Mr. Meredith's fine sonnet) the rank on rank of the stars struck Prince Lucifer that night he left his dark dominion, and his scars were pricked "with memory of that old revolt from Awe." Only that in this case the sense brought idyllic peace and a new wave of charm. Leaving fair Lynmouth to its slumbering delight, and high Lynton to its more breezy wakefulness, I had a curious sense of passing, not from a casual world-forgotten holiday haunt of a few days, but from an unspoiled nook where some of the happiest years of life had ebbed idly.

I feared the Caineyard no more.

CAINE! EVER AND ALWAYS CAINE!

The historian of nineteenth century literature will be as hard set to describe Mr. Hall Caine's life and momentum in the days succeeding "the Christian's" issue as he will be to describe that Scylla-cum-Charybdis tome itself. It is not too much to say that for many a trying day after that storm-charged 9th of August Hall Caine was the only man in England. As the wide walls of Rome in a famous epoch encompassed but one man, so the mighty Manxman seemed to expand as day succeeded day till with one foot on the little Manx strand the other might be said to rest by the German ocean, the corresponding fist thereto ready on the slightest provocation to stretch across the water and shake in the face of William II. himself. Or if the reader craves a less earthly metaphor, we might say that Hall Caine was the harvest moon in the English sky, and the faithful Robert Sherard (his literary factotum and interviewer-in-ordinary) a little star that twinkled obediently and proudly in its wake. Even Mr. Stead, who said that "the Christian's" hero was a failure as a Christian and not much of a success as anything else

(Et tu Brute!) was an ordinary and unconsidered individual for once.

Oh, the days of the Sherard dancing,
 Nice and neat to the Caineyard tune,
Oh, for one of those hours of madness,*
 Gone alas! like the "boom" too soon!
When the "pars" began to gather
 For the papers noon and night,
And the "Christian" orders startled
 Heinemann's heart with a wild delight.
Oh the times of the Sherard dancing!
 When the Manxman set the tune,
And the cats on the tiles of Greeba
 Chimed in answer under the moon!

And oh! the interviews and the proclamations! The world knows that a misunderstanding arose as to the Master's exact words to Sherard at the historic *Daily News* interview, so it was understood that in all succeeding ones expert reporters were stationed at Mr. Caine's feet, on his right hand and on his left, on the hearth-rug, on the door-mat, and at each of the four corners of the room, to take down the words as they fell from his lips, and thus guard against the recurrence of trouble or of trifling with history. It is also averred that the task of comparing notes after each interview was another "colossal undertaking," and that when it was over, the great novelist mopped his brow and wired to Mr. Heinemann: "This is an unheard-of business in Greeba Castle."

---

* In the ecstatic sense of course.

59

With only one typical episode of that memorable period may we dwell a little before passing from it for ever. The Master unbosomed his soul in the *Humanitarian* in the pessimistic wane of October. Let posterity note that his summer exuberance was stili royal and riotous. He still conveyed his revealings to us of the lower earth through the medium of the faithful and worshipping disciple, Sherard—Robert the wonder-eyed and the dutiful. There was a portrait of the great man facing the article. His legs were crossed and the forefinger of his marbly-white left hand tipped the boot of his right foot in awesome suggestiveness. What mystic symbolism was implied we knew not, but our fears were distressing. Marbly cold was the white face of his thoughtfulness, as Fiona Macleod might say: and his eyes had all the seeming of a wizard that was dreaming. They seemed to look on the old world going up in fire and the human race turned to spectres passing away to limitless outlands of night and wrath, while Greeba Castle alone stood where it did. Yea, we had not had such a thrill since the heyday of the Beardsley period.

And how shall I, with this sober, halting pen of mine, make plain to anxious readers the thoughts that breathed and the words that burned when the author of "The Christian" opened his heart to the author of "The White Slaves of England"? They went at once to colossal altitudes to study the great passions. Monsters these seem to me, but as tame white sheep of the fold were they in the eyes of the great Manx Shepherd.

60

There were only about half-a-dozen stories altogether, we were told, in which the great passions are
at play. (How many, by the way, had Mr. Hall Caine
already written?) Perhaps the greatest of them all was
the primal human story—the expulsion of Adam and
Eve from Eden. Reading between the lines we detected
a terrible suggestion that Mr. Caine would retell it in
a later realistic novel. "The highest aim of the novelist
is to tell the old stories in the environment of his own
time." And then, said the Master—and posterity can
fancy the thrilling flash in his eyes and the resonant re-
velation in his tones: "Don't banish the moral nude
from fiction under the impression you are thereby
banishing immorality." Yea, the head of Sherard bent
and his pencil trembled in a responsive inspiration that
recalled Mr. Morrison's at Loughton.

The Master went on to declare how wise people cried
"Melodrama" at the works of nearly every writer who
is *alive*, how in that sense "Hamlet" is an Adelphi production, "Othello" a Whitechapel murder put on the
stage; how he was absolutely opposed to the marriage
of convenience; how it was very likely that drink
would be the subject of his next novel; how he had
a very deep sympathy with the better part of the
Woman Movement; how he was sorry to think the influence of the Ibsen movement not altogether for the best.
—"It will be thought in the future that Ibsen was a
mad poet who imagined he was a man of the world"—
how, finally, amongst workers there was no impurity
rampant.

It may be that cold-hearted people can see no new or striking message here ; that they take as mean a view of Mr. Caine's social theories as did Mr. Saintsbury of his literary archievements. But to be great is to be misunderstood. Posterity will do him justice a hundred-fold. Posterity, too, will overlook the fact that Conan Doyle protested in the *Daily Chronicle* against his methods as a Boomster.

The end of this portion of his life-story was announced in the wane of the year, when, colossal soul that he was, yet his health gave way, and he was ordered four months' complete independence from booming and all other species of intellectual pursuits. The Great Christian went to Rome, and Byron's line :

O Rome, my country! City of the Soul

came instinctively to our lips. How Mr. Sherard would pass the winter in the Master's absence seemed a pathetic intellectual problem. We pictured him sitting isolated in that lonely courtyard at the back of the Author's Club, refusing to be comforted. He was sad to our mind's eye as Ovid or Dante in exile. We were all wrong. Like a certain cocoa, life to him was "grateful and comforting" even then. Indeed the quotation, as the reader will see, is singularly apt under the circumstances. Just as the Master had set sail we took up our new monthly magazines, and forth there fluttered a certain fly-leaf. It was a cocoa advertisement bill, and it gave us our latest glimpse of the literary work of Mr. Sherard. His portrait was in the corner.

In it he had the bland smile and the chubby air which come to all men, it seems, just after the cocoa-sipping stage. Mr. Sherard we read had found —'s cocoa "the very best," and "a real boon to literary men." When he was travelling the previous year, "Collecting materials for my book 'The white slaves of England' (Ah!) to many thousands I suggested such a beverage as yours." Since when, presumably, they "have used no other." Yes, that was the man who a month earlier was making the worth and the ways of Hall Caine crystal-clear to all men!

WHITE SLAVES.

(With apologies to Mr. Kipling.)

Where run your booms, O trimmer
  Of Caine's red Christian lamp?
Think not it is in Greeba,
  These doleful days and damp.
The White-Slave Ocean Horses
  Bear Hall far far from home—
The potent Pope of Manxland
  Health-questing goes to Rome!

Who's cast the spell upon you,
  Now Caine has set you free?
What drink is on your table?
  The best of drinks that be!
'Twixt tepid draughts and burning
  O, puzzled was my brain;
But now I've sipped Blank's Cocoa,
  I'll never doubt again!

63

What service have you paid them
  Who made it hot and strong?
To boom their boon I sent them
  A glowing note along.
And now it flies on fly-leaves
  From Pole to Pole that fall—
And say how slave the "White Slaves"?
  Blank's Brand has cured them all!

THE NEW DOOM OF NARCISSUS
(SOMETIMES STYLED RICHARD)

There was a fall of white marble in Richard's soul.
The morning post had brought no letter from Pauline.
He sighed, and turned with an elfin sigh to the bric-a-
brac of his heart, but in all the pieces his Arabian-
Nights' eyes saw nothing at the moment that he could
utilise for Bodley *belles lettres.* "Love for ever completes the world," he said mechanically, holding up his
pocket mirror with one hand, and with the other bring-
ing his gold-backed hair-brush to bear on the creamy
waves of his curls. "Love for ever completes the world ;
but Pauline is slow. Dear Pauline! Shall I ever see
her again?"

Pauline was the latest of the Golden Girls. He had
loved her now for two days, seventeen hours, and fif·
teen minutes. "Long, O absent rose of my heart, are
the cycles of love," he murmured as he lowered the hair·
brush, and·the glint of its back of gold went forth like
the sheen of Cupid's arrows through the window to lose
itself, he said, in one bubble of passion on the morning sunbeams' bosom beyond the Surrey downs. It got

no farther than the yard, where it died on the breast of a dilatory telegraph messenger.

The boy brought the telegram which told that Pauline was dead. Richard's sonnet on the dear little Bacchantes on her stocking (which he had stolen) had proved too much for her. The telegram said so, albeit gently. With a poignant iambic moan for lost love and wounded vanity Richard turned him over on his couch, and casting one last fond look into the pocket mirror in his trembling hand, he died.

Then some one wrote (à la Mr. Norman Gale):

> Come, Golden Girls, don't cry!
> E'en Dickies have to die;
>   For Love's a frisky fellow
>   Who rarely stays to mellow.
> Some lusty, log-rolled swain
> Will pinch your cheeks again,
> Send sweetly-scented notes,
> And steal your petticoats,
> When these fresh tears are dry—
> Come, Golden Girls, don't cry!
> Such grief is all-my-eye.

Before we follow the fortunes of Richard's spirit it is necessary to point out that the conditions of intellectual fame and of literary life altogether had become revolutionised at this stage of the world's history. To be a creative artist was quite a secondary consideration. The great point was to be "discovered"—for some intellectual eccentricity, or happy pose, or supreme quality of imitativeness, or amazing freak of intense and inconstant amativeness. On rare occasions the possession of a modicum of talent served the same purpose. The reign of the literary "discoverer" had become universal and unquestioned. First of all, Richard had found in the poets of the day a "composite Shakespeare": truer to their time than Avon's Swan, and possessing to the radiant seeing eye of the ideal logroller a something love-some and moon-sweet which Stratford's William had never boasted even in Anne Hathaway's eye in their courting days. Richard's neighbour, Mr. Grant Allen, had prided himself—more than Autumn sportman prides his bag of partridges—on his remarkable "first-sighting" of genius in unlikely and unlovely places. Mr. George Moore, when he could lift a gloating eye off the literary iniquities of Stevenson, had been similarly felicitous. Mr. William Archer, even in the thick of the fight for Ibsen, had sometimes found a moment's time to pause and shout across to his age that So-and-So should be booked forthwith (par grande vitesse) for the Immortal Isles. Mr. Lang, when no Celt nor Max Muller annoyed him, had his own uncanny discoveries. Mr. F. W. Robinson, expert investigators say, has never obtained his due as an unfailing and felicitous authority in that same Augustan Era of genius-exploration. Dr. Nicoll and the *Daily Chronicle* were at one stage so lucky in similar supreme lines that the question of the hour was where to find places in an over-crowded continent for their geniuses. Mr. T. P. O'Connor's "discoveries" were also manifold, but they were mostly of a peculiar feminine type, and were not always taken seriously, some allowance being made for Mr. O'Connor's susceptible and most sensitive gallantry.

Amongst them all, the "discoveries" of Richard stood out quaint and amazing. They shone with alarming regularity in his weekly reviews for a luminous evening paper of London. One day he welcomed the author of "The Laughter of The Stars" as a master of frolicsome pleonasm unexcelled since Shakespeare ; the next occasion his voice was a prose fancy of pathos compact as he saluted a new bard whose ruth suggested the materialising of all the tears ever shed of Mr. Stead ; as he hailed yet another—a sonneteer who had that glistening and palpable definiteness which the age had seen hitherto only in the theosophic lectures of Mrs. Annie Besant—his voice might be mistaken for the answer of the rose to the nightingale.

It came to pass as may well be expected that Richard's rivals in this art of intellectual "first-sighting" led him a troublous and dangerous time. Their pro·nouncements were as clanking armour when knight meets knight ; Richard's were as the flutter of frilled petticoats, and therefore his views were sweeter to an age that had been swathed in Mr. O'Connor's suggestive Books of the Week and the later fiction of Mr. Hardy.

The rival "discoverers" were driven by the force of circumstances to start literary journals of their own to carry on the war upon a colossal scale, to uphold their own several discoveries, and to curb the pride of such men as Mr. Hall Caine who were daily discovering themselves, or something more strenuous, more colossal, more subtly but gratuitously advertisable in themselves. All the traditions of the ensuing decade are of war and flame, the raging of fiery tongues, the flashing of sword-pens in the world. In old museums specimens of the paper's advertisement columns, and broken pieces of their delivery carts are still preserved. Very quaint is the antique wording : "Greatest Literary Discovery in the Universe." "Sighted at first glance more True Poets than any other Daily Paper." "Read the *Blazer* for the latest true Pilgrims to Parnassus." "Special Discovery Experts In All Parts Of The Globe." "*Bow-Wow* found out the Genius of Weeriwale six minutes earlier than any other Contemporary." "The Frills of a Golden Girl's Petticoat given away with Every Copy of the *Star-spangled Poseur.*" And so on and so on.

Duels, lawsuits and the clashes of many-phased conflicts smote the land. Nobody read much literature, few looked deeper than the cover of the latest volume printed, but almost everyone was a furious partisan of one discoverer or another. Special policemen were necessary on the farthing tram-cars to the suburbs to prevent portly and usually mild-mannered old gentlemen from tearing one another to pieces in support of their favourite papers and pretenders. Even Barry Pain was afraid to consider the question other than seriously. The assurance companies of the period issued special notices declaring that nothing would be paid to the next-of-kin of assured who met their deaths in conflicts arising out of questions of literary discovery.

Finally on a genius-exploration-syndicate-deal Mr. Hooley cleared a quarter of a million more money then he realised in the old days with Bovril.

Over weird and cloud-shadowed wastes had gone the released Richard. He thought of the over-praised line of Davidson's : "The waste, raw land where doleful suburbs thrive." "Only rose of my heart," said he, dropping unconsciously into the earthly jargon, "there are no suburbs." He sighed in vain for a suggestion of the Arabian Nights. There wasn't a piece of chiffon between him and the horizon. He was alone with a great terror. Some wondrous, incomprehensible force sent him on and on through the seemingly illimitable dusk. The solitude was appalling ; the sense of spiritual vacuum he did not mind so much. The presence even of Mr. Henley or Frank Danby would have been a welcome break to the horrid spell. He would almost listen without weariness to Mr. Jerome on Lord Salisbury.

He thought he had travelled for an æon, when suddenly he was brought to a standstill on the verge of the slow-lapping waves of an eerie ocean.

"O rose of my heart," he sighed with delicate deliberation, "is Pauline or is Nicolette beyond? And what does the morning star say to the moon?"

Mechanically he felt for his pocket-mirror, but that had been stored away with the days that were no more.

On and on with the great terror he wandered again —the same mysterious force sent him over the waters.

He stopped on a wild shore at last. He thought he had reached the home haunt of weirdness.

"I am as marble in flame," he murmured. "May there ever be a coquettish moon again, and a life with a mystical aspect of completeness? O sea, hast thou heard of the Twelve Golden-Haired Bar-maids?"

In another moment dark shapes and strange voices were about him. Then the dusk was lightened, for a cold white moon had arisen on the sea. It was so chaste that he did not look at it a second time.

A spirit came up.

"Richard," it said in a tone of infinite pity and pathos, "here are the legion disembodied spirits of the poets you discovered and log-rolled on your earth-world in your mortal life-time. Altogether they will chant their poems in your ears—every poem of any kind or grade or metre which on earth they wrote—and for ever you must listen."

"For ever!" wailed Richard as the great terror smote him and the chaste irresponsiveness of the moonlight hurt him.

"For ever! For ever!" replied the spirit, as the legion shapes gathered round.

Richard lay down on the dreary shore and moaned the moan of the lost.

He rose as the shapes had begun their appalling recitation. For the first time, on the hill rising statelily and gradual in front of him he noticed a troop of entrancing woman forms, dancing to and fro and fairer than Aphrodite on the old Hellenic seas. Lolling nigh them were two pleasant sinners whom he instinctively recognised as Omar Khayyam and Edward Fitzgerald.

"O roses of my soul, though *sans* paradises of chiffon," he exclaimed as he fixed his gaze on the woman troop, "may I ever draw near yon immortal consummation of all blisses? For they in sooth are the Golden Girls of All Girls."

"They are indeed the Golden Girls of All Girls," said the spirit above the din of the recitations, "but it is fated that you can never draw nearer."

The soul of Richard cried in iambic agony to the stars. The spirit was unmoved.

"Can you furnish me with a large-paper copy of my paraphrase of Omar?" asked Richard when he recovered; "do not say it is unknown in the everlasting realms, for has it not the hall-mark of Grant Allen, and was it not published by his nephew? I think the lines

> He sins no sins but gentle drunkenness,
> Warm-hearthed mirth, and kind—"

were emongst the neatest I ever did."

"The gods have no store-house for waste-paper," said the spirit briefly.

"May I even have a pocket-mirror and a gold-backed hair-brush?" moaned Richard in a soft slow metre.

"Never," said the spirit above the still wilder din, "and your face shall be on dusty days even as Paul Dunbar's poetry, and your locks shall be as Walt Whitman's philosophy. Even in the sight of yon Golden Girls of

All Girls you must be what the Celts call a holy show :
in other words as ugly as the literary morality of George
Egerton."

The ghastly din of the recitations drowned the
agony of Richard's lost cry.

A "*DAILY TERMAGANT*"
SENSATION

The editor of the *Daily Termagant* closed the door of his private room, as he bade his assistant editor take the vacant chair that stood opposite his own. The editor of the *Daily Termagant* was in a very reckless humour indeed.

"Can you suggest one likely plan that shall save the paper from the ruin that stares it in the face?" he asked drily, when the assistant had seated himself.

"I cannot, I am sorry to say," said the latter hopelessly. "You wouldn't listen to my suggestion that we should have a series of 'The Beauties of Marie Corelli' by Eric Mackay; 'Easy Lessons in Blague' by G. B. Burgin you also tabooed; you wouldn't even have Mr. Sladen's autobiography, and now he's gone and boiled it down for 'Who's Who.' I have worked—you know how I have worked—you know how our staff has worked. Our efforts have availed nothing. No one has any idea now that will stem the tide of bad luck."

"Don't be too sure," said the editor.

"Then again," went on the assistant, "you refused

74

those papers by that Vagabond Club man, called 'How the Modern Author Dines; What he eats, and What he would like to eat; what the Doctors say he might and might not eat; what he will eat and what he won't eat in the next century, and why; the influence of starchy foods on the progress of the sex-novel.' And so on. Why, with such a topic every author in the land would strike in and the boom would be amazing. When in doubt, play dinners, I say. Look at the Vagabonds, look at the Authors' Club! Feuds and pen-hatchets are buried under the table. The war-drum throbs no longer—when the dinner-bell has sounded; and the battle-flags are furled—at the unfolding of Literature's perennial flag of truce, the table-napkin."

The editor stroked his beard, and the flash in his handsome eyes made his pale but fine face look its best.

"We have been too brilliant and adventurous, Brown," he went on, "immeasurably too brilliant. We should have written like the lady novelists, or have been impertinent and vulgar. Fine writing is wholly out of place to-day. And I have no faith in the Club of the Lord of Sladen any more than in the Sword of the Lord of Henley. But—I'm not going to be cynical. Only a sensational move will save us now, and I'm going to make it. You may tell the whole staff that I shall require none of them to-morrow morning."

"Revolution, indeed!" said Brown. "Do you mean, Mr. Smythven that you can turn out a whole evening paper by yourself?"

"Nothing of the kind."

"Then do you mean to suspend publication to-morrow? In that case..."

"The second edition will appear as usual at eleven o'clock to-morrow. Most of the matter will, I hope, be got through to-night, though. Not a line will I write. My dear Brown, the next issue of the *Termagant* will be the people's paper, written and edited by the Man in the Street. This is our last chance. I'm having sensational posters got out; I'm sending displayed advertisements to all the big morning papers. And I'm trying to lug in a Buddhist motto or two from Sir Edwin Arnold. They always make English people laugh, for some inscrutable reason. Yes, the people's paper, written and edited by the Man in the Street and his brethren, will save us, or nothing will. My own impression is that it will make a tremendous sensation."

"I confess that I don't quite follow the idea," said Brown.

"Now, for many months," said Smythven, quietly, "I have been studying the letters and suggestions of a group that at first I thought persistent and intolerable bores. There's the score of different creatures who know how to manage the paper better than one's self; there's the amiable gentleman who has a mystic grievance against the Lord Chancellor; there's the genius who wants to regulate the law as to omnibus tickets; there's the sinner who sends you suggestions for improving on the whole scheme of the universe; the Camberwell tailor who has written an epic on the Last Judgment from an unorthodox point of view; there's the young lady who knows everything, has a bowing acquaintance at least with everyone's cupboard skeleton, and so dearly wants to write your society column. You have heard of them all.

"Well, I'll telegraph to everyone of them at once. They'll come to the office to-night. They'll have pens, ink, paper, and drinks. They can write what they like, and be hanged to them. It will all go in just as they write it. Also, Brown, you'll go out into the City, and, shrewd judge of men as you are, you'll pick out the neatest type of what we understand as the Man in the Street. Bring him here, too. He'll drink as he likes, and write as he likes. 'Twill all be printed. If there's too much stuff, they must decide amongst themselves what had better go out."

A little of the chief's quixotic fever caught Brown. A quarter of an hour later he was busy furthering the arrangements for the mad scheme.

At daylight next morning the assistant-editor knocked at the door of the editor's room. Smythven and the young lady who knew everything were engaged in an animated conversation. They had been subtly attracted to each other from the first, and their discourse on journalism and genius, affinities and newspaper perfection, had sounded very delicious keys (to them) as the hours went on, and the Man in the Street and his strangely-gathered brethren prepared the matter for the paper upstairs.

"It will be the most fearful and wonderful production

on which the eye of man ever rested," said Brown. "The drinking, writing, clash, and clamour upstairs is not surpassed by anything out of Bedlam. I've just glanced through the epic poet's copy, the button-hole reformer's copy, and the copy of the man who advances seventy-five reasons why England is going to the dogs, and I assure you that the gods had never such food for laughter."

The editor scarcely heard. The look of dreamy romance sweetened in his eyes as he looked across the table at the young lady who knew everything. How modest and bewitching the tender light in her young eyes!

At that moment the sounds of appalling commotion came from the upper regions. Cries answered cries, bodies fell heavily to the floor, chairs and tables were heard to crash, and Bedlam seemed to have turned and set to rend itself to pieces. The assistant-editor hurried away.

In a quarter of an hour he re-appeared. His face was white.

"We have had tragic work," he said. "They wrote too much copy, and the general opinion was that the epic poet should curtail his work by sixty cantos, and that the reformer of the human race should knock ninety sentences out of his peroration. They both objected, and a fearful fight took place. They are all wounded, and the Man in the Street is dead!"

"Good gracious!" cried the startled editor. "I'll certainly be held responsible for the trouble and the tragedy. I must fly this cursed spot. Bella," he said, turning to the young lady who knew everything, "Bella, you will fly with me?"

She glanced shyly at the jewels he had given her, blushed, and thought a moment.

"I cannot," she said, in her dear, demure way. "You see, my husband is expecting me. Of my three husbands he has proved the kindest, and I hate to desert him."

Smythven swept from the room with a curse. The police entered a minute later, and took possession of the office. The *Termagant* never appeared again.

A double number of *To-Day* appeared the following week. Mrs. Sarah Tooley described therein her interview with the young lady who knew everything. The facts she recorded of that memorable night in the *Daily Termagant* sanctum became the talk of London. They afforded Mr. Barry Pain a god-send in the shape of a new impulse for his "Smoking Room" philosophy— and for fully six months he worked it for all it was worth, till the faces of his readers grew Black and White by turns. As the cynical were wont to say:

> And Pain repeats himself in many ways
> Lest one bad jokelet should escape the world.

AUTHORS I CANNOT TAKE
SERIOUSLY

There is of course the colossal instance of Miss Corelli with her somewhat undisciplined mind, her capacity to make tempests of the trivial, her hysteria
anent the commonplace, and her parboiled soulfulness.
But—for all her insistence on the privacy of her personality and her sometime stormy protestations of
shyness—she has been so insistently before us for years
that even the intellectual have come to accept her in
that curious, unquestioning, half-unheeding way in
which some people accept a village beldame and others
the *Daily Telegraph.* We may go further and admit
that her sentimentality has been as a Mother Seigel's
Syrup to many a literary hypochondriac, that her characters have had in certain emotional and critically
unintelligent quarters an educational and quickening
influence second only to Madame Tussaud's. She has
sounded a warmer whoop than the *War-Cry's* in spirit-
ually forlorn backrooms and boarding-houses ; she has
carried a message, a sentimental sal volatile to many
a yearning domestic and Higher Harriet in that stage
when the *Family Herald* had begun to pall. In a vague,

stupid way, large tracts of Maida Vale and Brixton have accepted her as an inspired female ; a Joan of Arc on a tram-car. For these things, not without good in their way in a commonplace world the charitable historian has no heart to lay bare the Great Show of her quasi-literary absurdities. Besides they are long and life is fleeting.

Miss Corelli's half-brother, Mr. Eric Mackay, once kindly spoken of for the "Love-Letters of a Violinist" has added to the gaiety of nations by solemn tilts at brother minor-poets, by interfering once in a way with Silomo's or William Watson's settlements of the Eastern question, by the quaint fashion in which he prepared the way for Mr. Swinburne to take him gently by the ears and drop him over a precipice ; and finally by the unconscious humour of his own ambitious poetry. He shouts well. One can picture him as the good-natured, impetuous man in the street who throws up his hat with many a bold hurrah for England. This were well if he did it on gala days as a private citizen, but the freak of calling the Muses and the world to celebrate it and see it in a book shows a peculiarly defective sense of the eternal fitness of things. It has been unkindly hinted that in his tempest-tongued telling of the Empire's glories, and when his eye rolled most in fine frenzy, he still kept a modest corner of it on the Laureateship ; and in any case wounded must have been his faithful spirit when the doubtful gift went to mere Mr. Alfred Austin of Swinford Old Manor, where, as naïve interviewers have told us, a well-fed cow will look up in wonder—when the literary paragraphist appears; Mr. Alfred Austin on whose reputation Dr. Jameson unconsciously made a most damaging and damning raid; Mr. Austin whose place in poetry was dubious even before that sad event; Mr. Austin who sings of the obvious and cannot impart a consecrating touch to it; Mr. Austin a patch of whose "Garden" (dewless as he tells us under the dense oak in the most generous night) might be said to be typical of too much of his literary art. Yea, it was sad that in the filling of the office graced by Pye and Cibber, Mr. Mackay, whatever his private feelings, should have been ignored. Was it in vain that he sang tempest songs for England, and scarified other bards?

Shall I, the hero of a thousand shouts
    For tip-top England, to the background go?
Shall I be meek and modest, I whose flouts
    Have maddened Swinburne? Why, High Heavens! No!!

Sing ho! the day of Eric! England needs
    Not whining singers but a man of storm.
Shut up, ye little winds among the reeds!
    How dare ye whine the day *I* feel in form?

There is a very cannon in my throat!!!
    And wild 'twill boom for England. And the sea
And all the lands shall shudder at the note
    That thrills with tip-top England's destiny.

The very gods shall quake before I'm done,
    The "minors" shrink into their shivering shoes.
England e'en yet may fling her brave-tongued son
    The Laureateship, that darling of my muse!

I often wondered how Mr. Percy Fitzgerald could continue, as the years rose and fell, with his novels, his travel-tales, his autobiographies, his stage-lore, his Boswells, his Lambs, his lectures, and so on, ad lib. Thirty novels, twenty-five biographies, five autobiographies, a dozen stage-books, and Heaven only knows how many other things! Yet never morning wanes to evening that he seems otherwise than in the blithe beginning of his labours! Yet never morning waned to evening but some hardy bookmaking idea occurred to him. I have sometimes said to myself, in amazement at his energy : "There's the ideal man to place in charge of the stone of Sisyphus!" A picture of Mr. Fitzgerald appeared some time ago in one of Mr. Shorter's publications. Never since have I wondered at his labours. The likeness seemed to explain everything. There was a grim-weird-glory-of-going-on air about it which fascinated one : it suggested a sort of combined re-incarnation of the Ancient Mariner and Ulysses. He held us with a glittering eye which yet appeared to gaze into an eerie sunset region where the sun is always on the point of setting yet never sets. It is my solemn conviction that Mr. Fitzgerald will never die, and will never cease bookmaking.

One day in the nineties Mr. I. Zangwill went lecturing in Glasgow in the gaiety of his heart. Amongst his adventures in that fateful period was the introduction to a young University man with a taste for metaphysics and Mr. Meredith. The young man had written

83

a paper in which the Dreamer of the Ghetto detected uncommon power, and he said so. Mr. Zangwill was not conscious, perhaps, just then of the deep responsibility of the act. But the day came when that young man, who elected to be known in the literary world as "Benjamin Swift," published a book called "Nancy Noon," and we all knew the worst. We had scarcely recovered from the volume when Dr. Robertson Nicoll published Mr. Swift's life and times and portrait in the *Bookman*, and to the Hampstead Set and many beyond this their second, next-to-native Heath, was borne the great truth that another Brither Scot had "arrived."

I am afraid that I can give you little or no idea of the nature and purpose of this strange book in the space at my disposal. I should require this whole volume for the patient unravelling and the intelligible explanation of the turtuous life-threads that mingled, knotted, twisted, danced and played hide-and-seek in the story. And after all, my efforts would be in a measure vain. I feel that intelligible and matter-of-fact explanation would be a brazen insult to Mr. Swift's extravaganza-loving folk. I might as well try to explain sunbeams playing leap-frog down the Egyptian labyrinths, or the Courts of Puck and Titania making merry in the Catacombs. As for the tricks of language in the volume, the madness of March hares were bourgeois decorum in comparison.

Believe me, Mr. Swift put character enough and to spare into his book, and he has power also to spare, while for somersaults of expression you might confidently back him in any international linguistic Olympiad. My wonder is how he carries the mountain of affectation that the gods or ill-fortune have given him. Meredith, Meredith, thy disciples are more than we can bear.

The heroine goes out in Mr. Swift's second chapter to meet her lover on the moors in the songfulness of the glorious May morning. She fancies she hears his "Holloa," and "she has a stifled feeling at her throat." But, bless you, that is nothing.

"Ah me, the world's old roomy heart will find a place "for them, and its imagination will envisage this scene. "For the old loves of the old universes are all represented "here, the everlasting life of them and antique pathos. "Doubtless, also, there will be a more eager concern "when it becomes known that both he and she are pos-"sessed of a certain height of physical splendour that "has come to them through the generations. The apes "must surely be considered to have been working to "some purpose. For he who is standing at the top and "stamping the ground because of impatience is tall and "Titanic enough, altogether a man, it seems—nearer, "perhaps, the thirties than the twenties, but with the "mystery of youth, like a diaphanous cloud upon him. "Also he is dressed, I think, in some seemly hunting "suit. And she? The withered birch branches are "crackling under her feet as she ascends. And is that "her red kerchief down among the trees?"

> " 'Here comes the lady! Oh, so light a foot
> " 'Shall ne'er wear out the everlasting flint.'

"She is merely seventeen, the wonder of the village, "whose band of adorers will run to Earth's end to do "her hest: Nan herself. Her foot is already on the "moor. The sea is rolling eastward there; and it is "really a marvellous hour. And these are the children "of the Old, Old one, representatives of elemental "causes, children of a strange destiny. It is enough that "the dawn is shattering the night for them, and that "they are both vibrating with the unmistakable pulse "and vibration of rudimentary emotions."

They "had come out to fight love's everlasting battle, no matter what weather may fall. As if love will stand aside for even the traffic of the stars." The hero "shot terrible grapeshot of desire from his eyes!" also a fusillade of tormented emotions. Matters were apparently a little mixed, too, for the heroine was struggling in the mysteries of love, which happened to be a thicket. "She is caught in the thicket of it, and hears the snarling of the dogs, and is afraid." By and bye, in response to some assertion of her lover's, the cries "Never," with a flush on her face and a smile of unbelief. And what happens then? Hear her historian: "And at the word the grey-haired Everlasting Ironies ogled at each other." We thank thee, Scot, for giving us the phrase. You get this on the seventeenth page. And many a queer leap and turn of life and letters you get before the two hundred and ninetieth, where the author fills in his address which was then "Monte Oliveto, Siena," and writes "The End."

Mr. Swift called his second book "The Tormentor."

Presumably he thought of the title too late to bestow it on the first. This second volume possessed some eccentric brilliancy and an easy, elated habit of epigram. The epigrams occasionally appeared to grow tipsy. The characters were essays which in some subtle way were shot through a mould that made them look on the outside like human beings. Thus moulded they played their parts sometimes in electrical, sometimes in cometary fashion. Most of them were shot into an ice-field by way of finish.

Mr. L. F. Austin does not wish us to take him seriously. Mr. Austin poses as a very minor poet—in prose. He carries good humour, real and artificial, to fearful and wonderful extremes. In fact he is doggedly facetious. He is perpetually digging things in general and things in particular in the ribs, and politely asking them to laugh. Apparently nothing in the universe would be uninviting to his frolicsome knuckles—nothing from a pantechnicon to a comet. He is the weekly humourist of Mr. Shorter's *Sketch.*—Mr. Shorter, who has made the Brontës his own, looked lovingly after Victorian literature, and made momentous literary alliances with the living. Not the least momentous is that with Mr. Austin. To be sure with L. F. A. you have a subtle feeling that somehow you are getting humour on the hire system. He is a man of uncanny surprises, too. He asks you to-day to consider the beauties of Max Beerbohm, next week he is cycling through Weybridge, and the Martian in-vaders of Mr. Wells's fancy are hot and heavy on his handle bars; seven days later he belabours us with proofs that Hamlet, Prince of Denmark, was beyond doubt a vegetarian. His little jokes and free-hearted fancies he also devoutly treasures up, and succumbs after seven years or so to the demon of republication, showering the lot upon us again with wicked chortlings to himself. The author of "At Random" is Irish-American, but he has been tamed in London. On the whole he has been a quiet benefactor to his time. During the absence of Mr. Norman he has been assistant editor of the *Daily Chronicle*, but few of his jokes have been so serious as that. He would never make the mistake of Robert Barr, ex-Detroit editor, Indian chief, and humourist, the mistake of giving us the mild-cured blood-and-thunder of "Revenge" or a strike novel with a purpose, such as "The Mutable Many." Mr. Austin is more consistent.

Mr. Douglas Sladen is to my mind one of the most entertaining of all the figures which are in any wise potent with one of the Great Powers into which book-making London is divided. I know that by certain flippant critics his "Who's Who" is not taken either soberly or gravely; and the style of his *Literary World* reviewing, the trend of his "Dining Out" confidences in the *Queen*, are not always reverentially regarded. Yet Mr. Sladen's place is apart, is unique; and though he makes something of a humorous appeal to the slightly cynical student of our literary London, he is one of its most special products, a personality that simply cannot be ignored. None is keener than he on the festive side and significance of Literature. His "At Homes" have soothed long regions of book-making Suburbia, have warmed the cockles of the innermost sanctuary of its heart. Furthermore has he not done in his reviewing a more than great-hearted justice to the novelists who are dear to it? Those novelists have been called mediocrities, but mediocrities want human sympathy as well as most people, and since his return to London after his Melbourne professorship, his Japanese and sundry Oriental wanderings, a soft-eyed, broadly human kindliness and charity to intellectual mediocrities have been one of the high notes of Mr. Sladen's career. He has gathered a fold of them into his quaint compilation "Who's Who," where, along with the dates on which they honoured the earth by being born into it, the dates of their novels, their marrying and giving in marriage, he has religiously recorded the names and natures of their playthings. This bears us in sight of his *raison d'être* in Letters. That his subjects brought back the Hellenic or Elizabethan spirit is of less interest in his eyes than the kindly truth that some one or other of them has a fancy for the surreptitious collection of the neighbours' coat-tail buttons. That they admire Maeterlinck, that they follow Tolstoi, is nothing; an assurance that they like onions or play leap-frog is heavenly music to his ears; similarly in his capacities of joint secretary of the New Vagabonds', and honorary secretary of the Authors' Club, he studies with an almost pathetic solicitude the conditions of the Palate, and the daily developments of the appetites of Literature. Now the reader understands him : play and feast are his notes. He has felt the pulse, as it were, studied the teeth, and gravely regarded the tongue of the modern author in a manner so unique that we fear it must die with him, or become mere charlatanry through incompetent and unworthy imitators. In an age whose great thinkers were led to put forth the parrot-cry of a return to nature, he has not been afraid to stand out and bid our authors on the contrary to be of good cheer (in a dual sense), to come away from their fields, and folds, and retirements, to hie them to Whitehall Court, and be devotees for ever of the new faith of literary clubsomeness. To see one enjoying a beefsteak or honouring a toast with him, or facing his colleague Mr. Brown Burgin over an apple dumpling, would bring a light to his eye and a warm flush to his inner man, when the interpretation of Wessex or the creation of Sherlock Holmes would leave him cold. Nor are even these things the entire traits that mark him out from the thousand-fold book makers in our latterday London. He is the epic-hearted, seven-souled champion of literary damseldom and womanhood, an intellectual Launcelot to whom every bookish wench, or waif in petticoats is a Genevieve. Has he not written of the "sinewy" way in which some of them tell stories? Has he not also written—

"In an age in which women are marching to the
"front in the battle of life, no longer at a hysterical
"double quick-time, but with calm, dogged persistence,
."it is pleasant to see so many of them in the front
"rank of the literary battalion. Not to mention those
"who have long since won their spurs, like Mrs. Hum-
"phry Ward and Mrs. Burnett, we have strong women
"writers who are still quite young. * " (Gallantry! Gallantry!)

What graceful, felicitous phrasing! as if Romeo were
the critic and Juliet the leading novelist in the array!
What puzzles one a little, though, is the necessity for
the "spurs" in connection with the marching battalions.

> O Sladen, Sladen! our delight,
> Who like a fairy bland and bright,
> Dost move through mazy fields of style,
> A-sowing wisdom all the while.
> Hast thou thy flowery graces won
> In forests 'neath the Austral sun?
> Thy softer charms were found perhaps,
> In old days with the gentle Japs,
> The flavoured wit thou bring'st us home —
> Despair of Burgin and Jerome!
> We somehow seem to understand;
> What puzzles is the wonderland
> On éarthly or on lunar ground
> Where thou thy metaphors hast found.
> O Sladen, Sladen! our delight,
> In mercy speak and set us right!

When Mr. Stead stopped *Borderland* "for the present": pulled down the blinds of his great Psychic man-

---

* In the *Literary World.*

sion, as it were, and the question of the day was the future of "Julia," and men were asking if there was one supreme individual amongst them whom it was meet that she should still make the medium of her revealings, the thoughts of many turned instinctively to Mr. Sladen, the Champion and interpreter of the "spurred" and "dogged" onward-marching battalions of the fair sex. This thought for a season broke the poignancy of our sorrow for the loss of our beloved and uncanny quarterly. But for it indeed we would have felt in that doom-packed time as if we were looking at once on the going of the Gods from Olympus, the death-bed of the Graces, the Collapse of the Renaissance, and the grey, grim ashes of the cremated Beardsley period!

As a further example I am almost afraid that we must set that readable story-teller and honest-minded critical observer, Mr. David Christie Murray, amongst the authors who make direct appeal to our sense of humour. He positively meant, I fear, all that he said in his book "My Contemporaries in Fiction." It seems a wild remark to make, but the discussion that succeeded the volume's publication leaves little or no doubt that Mr. Murray really took his "Contemporaries" in that sober, earnest way he pretended!

It was not elaborate irony, it was not colossal make-believe. Serious! judicially serious! What an extraordinary thing! What an erring attitude! Mr. Christie Murray was not as wise as a namesake.

The shrewd publisher, Mr. John Murray, expressed

the wish some time ago, that for the next few years or so there should be a cessation of book-writing. Unlike Mr. Christie, Mr. John Murray was hardly serious, but in his facetiousness lay wisdom and a kernel of great truth. To take the contemporary book-world in its own grave way is to misunderstand its position. Literature positively wants a long holiday ; criticism needs time and means for meditation ; both crave the mountain breezes, the bracing, songful comradeship of the sea ; the exaltation of spirit, the enlargement of horizon which the ideal holiday—of soul as well as of body—brings. Truly here were silence golden. The Chosen People let the land lie fallow at certain periods ; even the Chosen People of literature—to say nothing of the neighbouring Gentiles—might treat similarly the regions of imagination and all art. Men and things in the book-world are most lamentably "run down," and we should not treat them as if they were riotously robust.

The question will have to be faced in all gravity some day. Cultured and intelligent people must surely grow tired of the volumes of ever lower and lower vitality, ever narrowing art, which are in courtesy or ignorance styled the "Books of the Season." They will make out a list of those of the world's great books of which so far they know no more than the names—and with the generality of people how formidable is such a list!—they will allot a few years to "pulling up" with those classics, and then, soothed, uplifted, freshened in spirit and widened in mind, they will think of asking if any contemporary has got anything immortal to say.

Meanwhile the publishers noting the "spirit of the time," will practically have ceased to publish anything new; they will tell the ambitious young man and the ardent young woman with manuscripts that "really the only market is for the Charing Cross edition of 'Epictetus,' the Mark-Lane 'Homer,' the Blackfriars 'Virgil,' the Fleet Street 'Dante,' and the rest of them. Before half-a-dozen of the Silent Years are over the multitude of those ambitious young men and women will be doing useful work with the steam-roller, and the sewing-machine; with collar-dressing, with sub-editing police-court reports; with market-gardening, and teaching biology to evening classes. By the end of the period of Golden Silence a young man or woman with a manuscript in Paternoster Row must needs be as strange as Macaulay's New Zealander. There will then be a chance for the rise and the quiet consideration of the genuine litterateur.

Assuredly such a happy time must bloom in some far, fair century forward. We cannot go on at the present rate of almost machine-making prose and verse, of flat, thin-spreading, air-beating criticism. Our minds rebel at the daily strain and the resulting dulness. We write and read a hundred books a month, at the lowest; we have read them at our burdened tables while the Spring blossoms burgeoned, and the Summer sang to the seas and lands, and the cloistral woodland aisles of Autumn grew sadder and dimmer, and Winter laughed wild and shrilly in the face of Time, and Nature had her myriad appeals and messages which we heeded not

—no, we stood "with blinded eyesight poring over miserable books"; muffled for us the music of the spheres. And lo! on our tables lie another hundred, and another—Grace in his heyday cannot make centuries like the publishers' messenger. And the difference between the new hundred and the hundred volumes we reviewed last month ʃo man may tell.

Yet, withal, we must candidly admit of course that if the creative spirit is denied to the vast majority of those in our midst who have assumed the masques and airs of litterateurs, they possess in many instances most diverting and unconsciously engaging traits. Though it knows not, the sides of literary London are splitting with laughter-moving material. Even a few great figures have been affected in an amazing degree by the peculiarities of their age, and losing awhile their intellectual sanity and severity, have played the fool agreeably. It is well worth while, even in an age that deems itself serious beyond all telling—an age that has deceived so experienced a traveller as Mr. Christie Murray—to lay down our classics for a span, and go out amongst the fancy fair of the freaks and try our luck at shooting literary folly as it flies. If we look with the right vision we cannot fail to see a whimsical rally, the Absurd putting on the airs of Art, Art putting on airs of the Absurd, the Non-essential walking as if it owned the earth and had cheated time into giving it a lease in perpetua, the Ephemeral solemnly making out and endowing its gifts upon Posterity. But to take them seriously—not this journey, thanks!

I cannot take Mrs. Sarah Grand seriously—as a novelist. In publishing this statement, perhaps, I have gone far towards blasting my literary career, for I fear I have greatly offended that great, good woman, Mrs. Sarah Tooley. Mrs. Tooley in all probability will go down the immediate ages as the biographer of royalty, but in distant æons she will surely shine out essentially, and it may be solely, as the interpreter of Mrs. Grand. Personally I can never forget that day in the dying '97 when it was announced to the world at large that Mrs. Tooley had had with Mrs. Grand "an important and deeply interesting interview." Verily my pen trembles as I recall that momentous proclamation. These supreme women had met! "The Heavenly Twins" (new series) had shaken hands and talked—it might even be their lips had touched! My sole wonder was simply that earth did not burst into one universal coat of blushing blossoms for joy of the moment and the meeting.

A little later I read "The Beth Book." A few hundred pages of its full five hundred have absolutely no connection with story-telling of any kind or character. Mrs. Grand has thought earnestly, though perhaps to no very great purpose, on a number of questions affecting the upbringing of girls, the training of the young idea, and the general condition and status of women in the modern world. She nags in a most inartistic way, but much though I dislike her method, I see, of course, the justice of a number of her—not very original or graphically put—pleas for womankind ; and I have no idea of setting myself to controvert her theories on the subject of child-management. But on the question of the number of pages which may justly be devoted to the subject in a novel I fancy I would differ directly and utterly from the lady. Mr. De Vere has said that poetry refuses to take up more philosophy than it can hold in solution, and surely something similar may be said concerning literature and the ethics of the nursery.

Mrs. Grand is concerned with two generations, and she follows Beth, her heroine, from her birthday through her infancy, childhood, school days, love affairs, such as they were, married unhappiness, revolution, and efforts in literature with tireless particularity. Of course a thoughtful woman dealing with so sensitive a heroine must needs be interesting at some stages. This is her summary of Beth, who was born in the north of Ireland, and was a coastguard officer's daughter : —

"Beth was a fine instrument, sensitive to a touch, "and considering the way she was handled, it would "have been a wonder if discordant effects had not been "produced upon her. Hers was a nature with a wide "range. It is probable that every conceivable impulse "was latent in her, every possibility of good or evil." Think of that!

The infantile and girlish progress of Beth in Ireland and Britain is detailed to very tedium. "She had a great aversion to bread and butter at one time." She duly discovered that there are two halfpennies in a penny. "She got a penny on Saturday, promptly spent it in sweets, and by Monday she wanted more." Really! Of such detail the early chapters are compact. Through mortal page on mortal page of them one is expected to travel. The trivial succeeds the ordinary till the heart cries. It is as if one stood on the platform at Ludgate Hill waiting for one's train to the green, human country, and was forced for a whole hour to wait and watch the passage of lumbering goods trains and intolerable coal-trucks. As for the style in those pages, it is sometimes ingenuous and sometimes curiously amateurish.

Decidedly a great deal of the matter in the book should have been put into a volume on the proper rearing and development of children, a second one on the management of girls, and a third one on questions affecting the woman of more mature age. Or much of the early portions might have been utilised in a series of lectures to an audience of mothers. Mrs. Grand strikes one as well equipped for the rather positive though perhaps unduly detailed opening of a discussion at such a meeting. Probably the other mothers present would have a good deal to say in opposition to her. But at any rate in such a place the matter would receive appropriate attention. Jumbling the material together as we find it here, and calling it a novel, is a further illustration of that amateurish idea of literature which meets one so often in the book. The sympathetic governance of the children's room, or young ladies' academy, is an admirable thing, but it is a poor equipment for the literary world. To be sure Mrs. Grand puts some childish fancies very well, and asks naive questions about the mind and the universe. But these are hardly enough.

In succeeding pages there are many womanly recollections, affecting enough and natural in their way, but certainly not touched by any illuminating art. Altogether, Mrs. Grand takes a long time to make Beth interesting; even then she goes on adding, fingering, and rearranging bits of character, pieces of peculiarity, glimpses of mood, like a collection of bric-à-brac. We see far too little play of real human drama. Mrs. Grand is well-meaning, but her method is laborious. As she pursues it the Muses take sal volatile, and the Graces go to sleep.

Humorous poetry of a dry and delicate kind permeated the work of Mr. Stephen Crane in his Green Badge of Courage period. In the eventful year '97, he discovered Ireland. He looked up to Queenstown on her high terraces and found her eminently contemplat·ive. Staring always at the coming and the going of great ships she sat. Her business was to witness. From her pride of place one could almost hear the voice of the western world, he said, and see the other millions. Hence Ireland here had a strange broad quality, a kind of egotism of vision (O Sage! O Sage!), as if from their hills her people could comprehend the gestures of a man in Denver. Because they were Irish, and because of this pinnacled position Mr. Crane discovered that they assimilated like lightning. When a stranger hove in sight they had a little accurate opinion, a mental snapshot, which was a perfect bit of machinery. We had heard of the "cloudy and lightning genius of the Gael," but "assimilate like lightning" was surely the artist's touch!

Mr. Crane went inland and discovered the Irish policeman. This Irish policeman was clothed in a light that never was on land or sea. His helmet flashed in more lights than Don Quixote ever saw in the barber's basin. Mr. Crane's Irish constable was a poetical, pensive, almost intangible personage who held no discourse with plain-clothes Pat and was unloved of Irish girls. Apparently if he talked it was merely "to fill up the blanks in life"—Mr. Yeats may have taught him Maeterlinck! Certainly his soul was like a star and dwelt apart. He was—in Mr. Crane's version—such a figure as we might expect John Keats to set in one of those

> Magic casements opening on the foam
> Of perilous seas in faery lands forlorn.

What a difference it might make in the relations of the two countries if we could only have Mr. Crane in Dublin Castle as Chief Secretary!

Mr. Leslie Stephen is a cultured and judicious critic, but at times he says happy things whose quaintness might well make old Saturn shake his sides. One day he stirs the envy of Barry Pain and Max Beerbohm by the solemn statement that Pascal was a sincere, an humble, and even an abject believer, precisely because he was a thorough-going sceptic. Another he discourses persuasively on the influence of fatness upon poetry, with illustrations from Shelley and Byron. These things are not to be enlarged upon in clumsy language. We enjoy them like the enlivening sunshine, thanking the gods for gifts so fresh in an age of prose and dullards.

THE GREAT MACLEOD MYSTERY

Fiona Macleod wrote of the Hebrides, and the first effect on the southern temperament was fascination. "The Sin-Eater" and "The Washer of The Ford" were of tragedy and glamour compact; they had a species of magic which some critics imbibed like wine. Fated ground seemed Iona and those wistful, spell-struck outer isles, with their tragic traditions, their blend of music, romance, horror and mystery. Still later her lyrics, "From the Hills of Dream,"—though the lyric appeared scarcely spacious enough for her talent, and lacked the atmosphere of mist and enchantment which in the wider world of the best of her stories was made memorable—her lyrics often were quick with beauty : beauty of moon-white shoon, of the fairy-footed grasses, of the shadows and spells of the moor-side. With uncommon art she even imparted a spirituality to a few milking-songs. To the beauty of romantic passion and the mournful beauty of woman's tragedies she also gave some striking, irregular song in which we still deemed something lacking. Somethng, too, in her poetry at times looked a mere beautiful juggling with mystical phrases, yet the former melody haunted her lips even when she had apparently no care to be intelligible. It might be reasoned that she was at such times like a woman of genius who carried the most ordinary woman's whims and caprices into her poetry. It could also be said that a little less of the influence of Walt Whitman—to say nothing of Mr. Meredith in his more tantalising modes—upon her wild Celtic power would be eminently desirable.

Thus far the voice of, let us say, criticism. A season came when London awoke to the fact that it knew not Fiona Macleod as it knew the great authors of the hour. Her appetites were a sealed book to it; the colour of her hair was more mysterious than any Northland mystery. A wild, almost Hebridean, hunger passed here and there through the literary world, a hunger for a feast of fact, even with a little that might be fancy-bred, concerning her stature, her wardrobe, her next-door neighbours and the desire of her eyes. The paragraphists were for once dumb oracles: a thing unprecedented in our all-revealing age.

Then elusive whispers stirred the land. Fiona Macleod was William Sharp; Fiona Macleod was William Butler Yeats; one confident but perhaps waggish voice murmured "T. P. O'Connor," thereby associating one further irony with the name of the bland and wistful Irishman who in middle age came to damn the four-pound loaf and glorify the neurotic woman. For many days and seasons the whole secret was a worry and a source of marvel in Fleet Street. Witness this plaint in a literary quarter of an evening paper, a plaint which seems to voice the spirit of a day when an interesting, yet to some minds almost tragical, announcemnt was sent forth :

"Another development of the great Macleod mystery!
"The Lady Fiona of Iona is now said to be married, and
"the hopes of certain imaginative young enthusiasts of
"the Celtic Renaissance are dashed to earth. Whether
"the young lady (for the adjective we will brave the or-
"deal by fire, water, or Kalyard dialect) should be de-
"scribed as Mrs. Macleod, or whether she was origin-
"ally a Miss Fiona Macleod, and is now a Mrs. Mac
"Somebody Else, we know not. The whole business is
"as mazy as that old dance tune, 'Miss Macleod's
"Reel,' and we appeal to the shade of Sherlock Holmes
"to help us out."

A resulting tragedy deserves at least an attempt in song :

THE BARD'S TRAGEDY

A Bard there was, and he twanged his lyre
(While prosing were you and I!)
To a book and petticoat and pen of fire
(With a mythic mamma, a nameless sire).
But the Bard he called her his Heart's Desire
(And Petrick Geddes * looked sly!)

O the dreams we waste, and the reams we waste,
And the moon-struck love we planned!
All offered to one who never could know,
Being either a matron whose pulse beat slow,
Or a Shade on Iona's strand!

---

* It is hardly necessary to say that Professor Geddes is the Celtic publisher and pioneer in North Britain. The Lady Fiona the was one of his bright particular stars.

His stamps he spent, and the reams he wrote
Were full of his weird love's cry.
A mystery fenced his Fair like a moat—
But a bard possessing the Celtic "note"
Must follow a Shadowy Petticoat
(Till the end of the world is nigh!)

O the flesh he lost! O his soul love-tossed!
O the jump from the bridge he planned!
When his dear Fiona some ruffian wrote
Was but William Sharp in a petticoat,
Or Yeats back from Fairyland!

But his foolish head he longed to hide
When a scribe that spurned a lie,
Proclaimed that his Love had been long a bride
(That her husband's eye was wakeful and wide!)
Gad! some of him laughed, but the most of him cried
(And he lay on his couch to die!)

But it isn't the loss, and it isn't the cross
Now burns like a Bodley brand.
It's coming to know that no publishing friend
Will print or pay for the lays h penned
To his Love on Iona's strand.

GALE'S OWN MIXTURE:
A FIND FOR THE AUTOLYCUS
OF NINETEENTH CENTURY
CRITICISM

Mr. Norman Gale plays cricket and football, I have learnt from his daily biographers, and Mr. Le Gallienne and others have assured us that he has written some of the bright particular poetry of his epoch. I have never seen Mr. Gale at cricket or football, and, exhaustive though my researches have been in contemporary literature, I have unfortunately missed that work of his which could be called poetry. I am, therefore, unable to say anything about him in what are, perhaps, his greatest *rôles ;* but I have followed with delighted interest some of his boyish gambols in what he no doubt deems the field of criticism. In the *Literary World*—an organ popularly supposed to be concerned with literary criticism, to say nothing of the quaint intellectual confidences of Mr. Douglas Sladen—he has dealt with Mr. Morley Roberts's "Maurice Quain.*"

---

* This is of course an 1897 volume of Mr. Morley Roberts ex-miner, traveller, story-teller, and member of the Authors' Club.

and the sight out-Rugbys Rugby (pardon the present tense—I cannot escape it—the whole scene is so vividly before me). It is criticism of the whoop and yell, the triumphant "goal," and the flying football. It imparts into *belles lettres* the delightful boyish tame-savagery of the sporting field. As one studies Mr. Gale in his bounds and leaps and springs, one is tempted to cry with the wild character in Lever : "Clear the way for the Royal Bengal Tiger."

Mr. Gale begins with a fine burst :

"Mr. Roberts flatly refuses to allow bystanders to "note with an unperturbed mind the fluctuations of those "scales which on one side contain the hero of this novel, "and on the other no less a person, or sprite, than Lon- "don's Bad Angel. Mr. Morley Roberts, sometimes "with a spring, sometimes with a hop, and sometimes "with a jump, keeps on perplexing the measurement "by flopping in to the balance which holds the Bad "Angel."

Graceful, is it not? And luminous?

We discover, furthermore, that the hero, "strangely depleted of bread and cheese energies," was concerned to "hide his talents in a napkin." And then—I beseech the reader to brace himself for aboriginal things :

"The author has attempted to surround his whim- "sical, moody, savage puppet with an atmosphere deriv- "ed from an amalgamation of most that is gross, cor- "rupt, and barbaric in London. The idea is good ; the "coupling is a triumphant success whenever Mr. Mor-

"ley Roberts is content to play the part of a discreet
"chorus, but when he puts on Maurice Quain's trousers
"and necktie, and utters for himself what should have
"proceeded direct from the lips of his creature, we be-
"gin to perceive that the writer is guilty of assault and
"battery upon our sense of artistic proportion."

I think all this should have had artistic illustration :
the mind recurs instinctively to the author of "Pre-
historic Peeps."

The evolution of the "moody puppet," the reader
will have noted, is singularly interesting. In the "scales"
and the society of London's Bad Angel there is an attempt to "surround" him with a barbaric atmosphere.
The "coupling"(!!!)—of the puppet and the atmosphere—is a success when Mr. Roberts plays the part
of a "discreet chorus"(!) (As if Mr. Santley and his
pupils were to conduct a concert while they grappled
with Chatham and Dover cattle-trucks!) ; but all's a
muddle when he puts on the puppet's trousers and
necktie, and starts talking. In faith I cannot wonder.
There has been no more delightfully delicate blend
of metaphor since Addison wrote :

> "I bridle in my struggling Muse with pain
> That longs to launch into a bolder strain."

And Addison had nothing of our terrific modern
strenuousness !

But in "Gale's Own Mixture" there are other ele-
ments. I must quote a little further from this buoyant,
boyish review :

"Suffice it to say that whoever may nurse in his

"breast an unlimited love for our capital will surely
"experience an astounding attack of the staggers,
"while, with eyes unconsciously apeing the gooseberry,
"he reads the knock-me-down sentences to be found
"'scattered among the pages of 'Maurice Quain.'"

The moody atmosphere-coupled puppet subsequently went out in a boat on the river, became a
"fisher of woman," and was troubled about "the housing
of his catch." I am really afraid to proceed further.
Those quick changes and amazing developments are
too much for me. I have an uneasy feeling that somebody or other turns into an ape or a dragon of the
prime before the end is reached. If the Muses had
been visiting Mr. Gale before he wrote this "criticism"
they must have gone direct from a ladies'—I beg
pardon, goddesses'—athletic tournament on Olympus,
a tournament which ended in a scrimmage, and wherein
all things got mixed.

THE PASSING OF THE POETS

I once ventured to suggest that the prevalence of minor song in our day—"like a whole sea overhead," in Browning phrase—might be in sooth a sure sign of the Millennium. The cynics, no doubt, will treat the suggestion as sarcasm. Yet it could be honestly defended. We might reason this way: The world has grown many degrees sweeter and more musicful of late years; a wonderful change has come over the spirit of her dream, and the indices of that change are the despised minor lyrists. If the course of song continues to grow for the next hundred years as it has grown within the past decade there can be few save lyrical and sweetening influences in the universe. "The old world has gone up in fire," says Natty Cramp to his frightened mother in Mr. Justin Mc.Carthy's "Dear Lady Disdain." Who knows but that flowing minstrelsy, not fire, will be the new regenerating element—that some fair day to come the old earth will glide into the perfect new in a flood of entrancing song? Minor poetry may have a far deeper significance than the critics have attributed to it so far. Q. E. D. We may bid Mr. Traill be of good cheer on his lonely, frost-bitten high peak of *Literature*.

I am a few years older now than when I made the suggestion, and I have lost faith in my theory. I fear me that the most optimistic seeker after poetry cannot grow enthusiastic over its main tendencies nowadays. Mr. Traill's discovery of sixty several personages who spoke the language of poetry is as elusive as a New Atlantis or Mr. Yeats' Celtic Paradise, and it is to be feared provokes little else than hollow or good-humoured laughter amongst the serious or critical-minded at this time of day. One's spirit, the bitter-minded say, must have shrivelled overmuch if it can rest satisfied many moments over the slow fires represented by the poetical souls of at least forty of Mr. Traill's sixty. Mr. Stopford Brooke's contention that our men of verse for the most part are merely people who are keeping alive the habit of poetry seems much nearer honest criticism, criticism which frankly faces the truth, which recognises that in the world of song, as elsewhere, the body without the spirit is dead.

Poetry, to be sure, is illustrating few of the violences, revolts, robust crudities that have or had place recently in prose. Marie Corellis are far to seek in it. There is therein little washing of the soul in the gaze of all men and hanging it out to dry like clothes on a clothes-line. There is more artistic reticence amongst the poets than amongst their brethren in prose. Much of this unfortunately is explainable on no better ground than that of low vitality; that is to say, low spiritual vitality— vocal vitality is not so scarce. Yes, the spirit for the most part has gone, or is going, out of English poetry. The strong singers have sung their best, and those who pipe now that the greater voices are failing have not spirituality, vision, inspiration, realisation of life sufficient to lead them to large utterances and large effects. Skill of form and skilful echoing of old habit, the clever imitative song they possess and offer, but new temperaments, new reaches of spirit and imagination, new artistic surprises—they have them not.

The strong singers have sung their best. Mr. Swinburne, Mr. Aubrey De Vere, Mr. Meredith, Mr. Buchanan, Mr. Austin Dobson, Mrs. Meynell, Mr. Watts-Dunton,—the work by which the just will judge them seems as far back with the past as the work of Rossetti, William Morris, and Tennyson. *The Devil's Case* may go to the curiosities of literature, and the *Tale of Balen* is but an aftermath, meagre beside the *Poems and Ballads* and *The Songs before Sunrise*.

Almost all along the line there is a painful tendency to narrowing ways, to intellectual shrinking. Spiritual-mindedness and visionary power are becoming farther and farther to seek in the latter-day muse. This is largely explained, of course, by the fact that a number of more or less accomplished people who have none of the poet's inborn gifts and inspiration, who have acquired only the tricks and forms of singing, try to juggle with the art of poetry. The gods from their far-off Olympus have charged our modern atmosphere with a sort of intellectual electricity, and all who are more or less sensitive to such influences have been deflected to song or story by its currents. If one individual were dowered with all he might possibly be a genius, but the modicum each possesses under present circumstances rather tends to make him ridiculous, all the more so, if he puts on airs of immortality, as some of us are wont to do. A little inspiration is a dangerous thing. To use a more homely and, perhaps, a truer metaphor than that of the intellectual electricity, it may be said that a huge number of us are simply literary socialists. We have scant belief in, we have scant respect for, private property in literature. The ideas of the ages near and far, we regard as a sort of common fund from which all may take, simply dressing up in our own petty way that portion which we are pleased to draw from the great central store.

Certain poets seem to have been frightened from their first path, or chilled upon it by the coldness, preoccupation, materialism, and decadence of the age. Others, who have tried to be the singers of decadence, to pat and pet it in all its moods and emotions, have become unreal, or sorry, or cheap and nasty. One grows tired of their pipings about mean sins and timid indecencies. We agree with Max that they are not strong enough to be wicked. One need not be a "canting moralist" to despise them. One forgave Mr. Swinburne much of his early erotic extravagance and glamour of exuberant passion for the sake of his high-sweeping poetry ; but when we drop—after many palling stages this low-toned decade—to Mr. Wratislaw's *Orchids*, and the musical melancholy with which Mr. Dowson recalls his "old passion" (though we give Mr. Dowson credit for a few more than promising verses), well we are tired—that is all.

> "And thou, sweet Poetry! thou loveliest maid,
> Still first to fly where sensual joys invade."

Goldsmith was right apparently.

Mr. Richard Le Gallienne, in a much discussed article some time back, gave eight writers, if I remember rightly, as typical of latter-day poetical art. With a touch that would be Shawesque were it ironical, he subsequently dubbed them a composite Shakespeare. These were Mr. Davidson, Mr. Watson, Mr. Francis Thompson, Mr. W. B. Yeats, Mr. Arthur Symons, Mr. Kipling, Mr. Norman Gale, and Mr. Alfred Hayes. Obviously we must add Mr. Le Gallienne himself. Does not the list show at a glance the "wonderful" nature of our time of song? The plaintive bleating of midland sheep in the quiet evening is often suggested by the verse of Mr. Hayes in the *Vale of Arden*. Mr. Gale has become as thin and mechanical as Mr. Kipling and Mr. Davidson in their least interesting moods.

I hope it is not blasphemy to assert that Mr. Kipling and Mr. Davidson *have* uninteresting moods, for in many respects they are greater than even our great young men. They know more about the Everlasting Hills than Canon Farrar or Dr. Parker. Mr. Davidson's old habit of taking his worst characters to Heaven, and making God set them in the high places, all questions of the Decalogue being superseded for a homily of Mr. Davidson's making, is still with him in all its force in those hours when he is not engaged in the desperate effort to whip his humanity out of its dour suburban pessimism into cheeriness. Mr. Kipling, in such developments as "The Last Chantey," or when he is free for the nonce from the exacting duties of his poetical Colonial Secretaryship—takes a kindred high hand. The initial idea is a fine one, founded on the momentous saying, "And there was no more sea":—

Thus said the Lord in the vault above the Cherubim,
Calling to the angels and the souls in their degree,
    "Lo! Earth has passed away
    On the smoke of Judgment Day;
That Our Word may be established, shall we gather up
    the sea?"

No poet need ask a larger or sublimer subject for his song than that which here meets Mr. Kipling. The fact that he thought of it, and the further fact of certain lines in it, form a triumphant answer to critics who refuse to take him seriously, or who shake their heads over him as the established poetical superstition of the Man in the Street. But the treatment of the idea is unworthy of a poet of a spacious imaginative gift and that spiritual-mindedness without which the great poet does not exist. Thus, Judas and Paul having spoken to God, we have this strange turn:—

Then said the souls of the gentlemen adventurers —
Fettered wrist to bar for all red iniquity;
    "Ho! we revel in our chains
    O'er the sorrow that was Spain's,
Heave or sink it, leave or drink it, we were masters of
    the sea!"

Apart from the pert vulgarity of the concluding line, it argues a "little" idea of the conditions of things on the Judgment Day to represent a band of poor spirits hurling at the Father of the Universe a pitiful rendering of a nineteenth-century Navy League motto. Attitudes like this show how lacking is Mr. Kipling still in some of the higher poet's essentials; how he is apt to stumble when he leaves off idealising and poetising Tommy Atkins, and looks inward on his own vision and imaginative equipment.

Perhaps the very generous reader will think that a few casual attitudes from Mr. Davidson and Mr. Kipling are insufficient to justify any real charge of that small ungodliness or God-belittling spirit in which Mr. Buchanan is the chief latterday reveller. Somehow, the matter seems to me to lie deeper than that generous reader thinks, and concerns us chiefly—for, of course, a man's religion is none of our business—because it indicates not only a want of vision, but a remoteness from the great and moving realities of life. Mr. Kipling and Mr. Davidson, standing apart from the world, are not greatly enough equipped to depend on their own innate resources, and as time passes we seem to detect in them a spiritual shrivelling and narrowing, which explains some of their insufficiency and weakness, though this is accompanied in Mr. Kipling's case by a tremendous bodily and vocal vitality. With this state of things God gradually becomes a minor personage; if the reader will pardon the apparent profanity, a mere Celestial representative of John Davidson and Rudyard

Kipling who treat the archangels with an immeasurably smaller share of consideration than Mr. Archer would accord to a rival interpreter of Ibsen. It is wrong to ascribe their attitude towards Providence as kindred to that of Mr. Swinburne, who, in the moods of revolution and tempest-music which gave us "Songs Before Sunrise," declared that God was played out. That was one outcome of the furious extravagance of a brilliant mind ; of a soul whose genius was running in a lava-tide. The other which we have been considering is the outcome of a much poorer state of being. "But," cries the indignant reader, "have not all our great critics exhausted the language in their laudations of Mr. Kipling's amazing vitality?" Precisely, my friend ; but I am dealing with spiritual as distinguished from vocal, bodily, and other species of vitality.

But let us come close to Mr. Kipling. Do we not find that he is giving something to Imperialism which was meant for mankind? He fashions very bold and resonant stanzas ; he brings his clenched fist down as he shouts forth fine national sentiments which the Average Man will vigorously applaud and immediately forget. Some of this well-stamped, strong-thumped song-fashioning is as mechanical as barrel-churning ; as to finding artistic beauty within it, a large imaginative soul beyond it, one might as well expect to find violets blossoming on a blacksmith's anvil. It is good, bluff, straight-flung poetry for the "Ordinary Person," it will nerve him at his work, and on his platform, and by his bar ; it will make him a better, though a more insular, fellow ; but it will hardly blow the dust from any long-closed chamber of his spirit. (Some of it, by the way, cannot be understood by the Man in the Street, and at bottom it is so trite that no one else can appreciate it.) It is good vociferous poetry for its day and its generation ; but it requires no great gift of prophecy to say that the time will come when it must needs be as effete as the Corn Law rhymes or last year's reviews. In other moods Mr. Kipling sings with equal verve of power and force ; the might-is-right theory in sounding verse. A fine, though rough and long-winded example in "The Seven Seas" is "Mc. Andrew's Hymn," wherein the dour Scotch engineer, who says little and thinks much, sings the Song of Steam. The romance and miracle of ship and train Mr. Kipling sings gallantly once in a while. Indeed, Force, Imperial England, and Romance, are the guiding themes to which he gives his heart— and often heartening, though now and then raw and rugged utterance—and occasionally rather obscure utterance. In such pieces as "The Last Rhyme of True Thomas," and the poem about English Flowers in his latest volume Mr. Kipling looks into his real spiritual land, passing down a golden vista where the Man in the Street will hardly follow him. Such a departure proves to me that Mr. Kipling has an artist sense which he has but slightly developed and for which he gets little credit, that he is a poet who could write of the revealing heart of things as well as indulge in the whoop-and-drum-beat exhibitions, and the melodious-cum-mordant glo- rification of tame savagery and rude strength which have made his name and fame with the Man in the Street.

Yes, we get all too little of that better, artistic Kipling. He has been subjected to a good deal of spoiling of late years and seems to take to it kindly and unsuspiciously. Some time ago we found he was to figure in the costly, limited, elaborate "complete" edition with which the interprising publisher endeavours to give a classic air to the contemporary author, the "complete edition" which seems to be the Literary Earth-Heaven of the great young man. Mr. Meredith certainly, Mr. Hardy possibly, may deserve, and can stand, that sort of thing. One smiles when such an honour is accorded to Mr. Barrie, knowing that it will be taken seriously in no literary centre beyond the *Bookman* Office ; but in Mr. Kipling's case it may well set one's teeth on edge. Mr. Kipling is so young yet, in some respects so intellectually raw, in certain others so really dubious! The thoughtful critic cannot regard him otherwise than as a young man with much of his way to make, and with much of his way in doubt. A "complete edition" of his books, as if setting his own seal on the idea that his permanent work is done, and that his place henceforward is the slippered ease of the fireside, has altogether a comical significance. If this is not the idea ; if author and publisher really believe that, come what may hereafter, he has already done enough to warrant the costly and sedate tomes which denote in some minds the "contemporary classic," then the lack of humour and critical acumen is lamentable.

118

Give Mr. Kipling fair play, set him doing his best, and he illustrates skill, insight, grip of realities, and bold promise. Years ago, in the "Departmental Ditties," with all that was fortuitous and flimsy therein, the singer showed a genuine sense of the essentials and fine loyalties as well as the ironies of life. People who expressed surprise at the note in the '97 Jubilee "Recessional" had apparently forgotten, or had missed, his '87 Jubilee warning—for such it was—"What the People Said." The jubilations and congratulations were to him "The voice of the wind of an hour."

> Then, far and near as the twilight drew,
>   Hissed up to the sorrowful dark
> Great serpents, blazing, of red and blue,
> That rose and faded, and rose anew,
>   That the Land might wonder and mark.
>   "To-day is a day of days," they said,
>   "Make merry, O People all!"
> And the Ploughman listened and bowed his head:—
>   "To day and to-morrow, God's will," he said,
>   As he trimmed the lamps on the wall.

*
* *

> And the Ploughman settled the share
>   More deep in the sun-dried clod:—
> "Mogul, Mahratta, and Mlech from the North
>   And White Queen over the Seas—
> God raiseth them up and driveth them forth
> As the dust of the ploughshare flies in the breeze;
> But the wheat and the cattle are all my care,
>   And the rest is the will of God."

Now this is a true note, just as "Recessional" is ; an implied reproof to much of the vain vaunting and glorification of material externals of which Mr. Kipling himself has been laureate-in-ordinary on many occasions since. But just as it heartened us, we learned of that painful comicality of a "complete edition." May he find grace! It were a literary tragedy that the possessor of Mr. Kipling's virility and individuality should be led by the claptrap critic and the Man in the Street to content himself with Navy League rhymes and other manner of necessarily temporal and ephemeral things, too many of them appealing not to the spirit in us, but the tame savage. He must take care that the concluding sorrow of his "Merchantmen" may not come to have an expressive personal significance.

Let go, let go the anchor—
    Now shamed at heart are we
To bring so poor a cargo home
    Who had for gift the sea!
Let slip the great bow anchor;
    Now fools were we and blind—
The worst we took with utter toil,
    The best we left behind!

Mr. Davidson is apparently in a sort of transition stage. Beyond the want already mentioned in his work the only salient thing to be said about his late offerings, such as "New Ballads," is that they number very few which at all continue the better traditions of his singing. That shrivelling, half-living sense before indicated, strikes us with an uneasy feeling through the rest. The dim, aloof, semi-vital air of the suburbs glides coldly across it. In the good poems and the middling poems one can see that Mr. Davidson is well-meaning, that his lines are straight, that his heart feels honestly, that he is on the side of love, the finer, healthier senses, that his eyes are set toward the Golden Age. Still, his general work does not suggest the poet who has fully found himself, or who is in the way of going far. It has no great spontaneous well-springs of emotion, no artistic surprises, no impressive imaginative background. He drives his heart and his poetic impulses into a few strong things, and then he simmers slow. Sometimes one cannot feel quite sure whether the explanation is that he has large capacities unused yet, and is not quite decided as to his next departure, or that vision and spirit have done quite as much as they can be relied on to do—at any rate, till some new influences, some plunges into the heart of more vitalising life have flooded them with a new richness. Thus, although the few things indicated are real themes for praise, and make for betterment and light, the general quality is by no means reassuring as regards Mr. Davidson's poetical future.

The talent of Mr. Symons is undeniable ; however he may trail poetry through the music-hall, he has the sensitive gift and grace of the singer ; as Walter Pater saw he is "a poet with something to say ;" but in that musical, indiscreet, yet delicate art of his he is somewhat unequal, and his poetical mission still is unfulfilled, incomplete, not without a sense of uncertainty. Sometimes his art strikes us as artistry proceeding in its accomplished way without a fundamental basis of genuine vitality and compelling passion : but at other times passion takes wistful and beautiful guises in his verse.

Mr. Watson is still more of a manner than a mind— "The Purple East," perhaps, apart—more of the philosophical critic than the poet. Some of his work is not so much poetry as a poet's talk about poetry, more of it just what a true singer might say when the great passion was gone and only the afterglow was with him. Yet more suggests evening's coolness, fading of light and fire, and melancholy ; not the great, chastening melancholy of the masters, but a melancholy which is earth-cold. With all his well-carven work, his dignified, polished, scholarly mould, his ability to drop with little effort into the language of poetry, his power to dignify triteness of thought by an almost classic expression, he does not usually afford the impression of one who possesses a strong fount of intellectual vitality. His opulence is rather of the outer habiliments than of the animating essence, the soul, of poetry.

Mr. Yeats has lately toyed a little with the decadents, and I hope has found that this would never do. He has a sweet, wizard lyric gift, a delicate sense of beauty, glamour abounding. His genius to be sure is more like a haunting Isle of Voices than a comprehensible world. The passing winds wake him to eerie, charming music, but the English nature cannot grasp him as a substantial presence, a thing with views, appetites, a code of philosophy ; he is to it a disembodied spirit, and Mother Albion does not care for disembodied spirits. If Mr.

Yeats could go into Parliament, or edit *The Daily Chronicle*, or launch a newspaper syndicate, he would be a much larger figure to his age. But happily that is impossible ; and so he remains an undisturbed, serene, haunting singer for the few.

Mr. Yeats' faults are chiefly the tendency in his quest for strange beauty to treat truth as a minor consideration ; to use the fairy and sheogue symbols overmuch, and often in his pursuit to look upon the ground and into the clay a little too intently. It is comprehensible, but the idealising of the weak worm, the field-mouse, and the rats by the oatmeal bin is not always interesting. In "the poor foolish things that live a day," it is well to see the vision of "Eternal Beauty wandering on her way," but mayhap even one of the truest of our poets may carry his theory of mouse-magnificence rather too far.

Mr. Yeats' song has at any rate the air of inevitableness. With a number of his contemporaries, on the other hand, you feel that their singing is more or less accidental, the result of passing coquetries and experiments in one life-phase or another, rather than the outcome of the deep, unsounding, unchanging nature. Pagans, pessimists, decadents, cynics, satirists, they are to-day, but it is easily felt and seen that they may be something else to-morrow. Dealing with the tendencies of latterday poetry, and making these gentlemen the basis of the study and the verdict, would be taking them too seriously, and trusting on very shifty premises into the bargain. All we may say is that they keep to narrow ways and limited spheres, that they essay many small parts of life but never a coherent view of the whole; that they seldom see much beyond the externals of things, that the body rather than the soul is their province; that they lack staying power, and seldom or never expand; that they are rather Life's slaves than vital, plastic, creative artists who can mould Life to their will. They reach Olympus, scale the heavens, ride the chariot of the sun, and hear the music of the spheres no more; they ride on 'buses, and are drear with the sense of drab-environed streets. Some know no more of the world than Clapham or Bloomsbury: when they go abroad they carry Clapham and Bloomsbury with them; they see the outer world with city and suburban eyes, and when they return it is still with Clapham and Bloomsbury, and nothing more.

There are exceptions. One young singer has come before us of late whose outlook is larger, and whose sympathies are deeper. Mr. Stephen Phillips one day sang, however unequally, the epic hopelessness of Hades, and on other days the larger Hades of monotonous modernity, with its murder of spirit and feeling. And a world tired of narrow grooves, and limited, feeble songs, has given him its meed of praise very heartily. Mr. A. E. Housman, with his kindly and pensive sequence of trills called *A Shropshire Lad*, bore us back by homely country ways to simplicity and a region of the heart, and we were grateful. In an age of much individuality and rich creativeness, Mr. Housman would mayhap receive little attention, though he would please any who noted him. In our *blasé*, bourgeois period he is a distinct possession.

Apart from these, and little recked of by the complex contemporary world, Mr. Bridges goes in staid dignity, restoring and imparting a sense of majesty to an art that has much need of it. Mr. Lionel Johnson follows with a grave, solemn, austere, and academic spirit, whose stately grace is softened once in a while by a lyrical, Celtic current, and a sudden wistful longing for the green, glowing world in the distance beyond University ways and cathedral aisles. Such singers, though the additions they have made to original poetry are not great so far, yet have done something to keep poetry dignified and reverend, lofty as the masters left it, worthy of an age which had seen Newman and Pater, Patmore and De Vere, and their kindred. Mr. Francis Thompson, with all his inequalities, has done something similar, though fitfully, unevenly, at times violently. Spiritual and imaginative opulence Mr. Thompson possesses ; it over-runs his pages, as in *Sister Songs*, like a lava tide, producing havoc of form and some unprofitableness of thought, casting around confusing ashes of sentiment and barren blocks and boulders of words. Yet warm and heartening is the tide of emotion, though the artistic result has often a post-volcanic appearance. A flippant lady wrote the other day an excusable story of two or three men who taught a dog to understand print and by a neat arrangement to write out his impressions. He grew intellectually haughty, but died in a fit of depression and chagrin because Mr. Thomp-

son's poems were beyond him. That I fear is the philistine's and the average man's attitude. I do not know
that this clever dog would have fared much better with
Mr. Thompson's "New Poems," for though therein
sweet fancies fall in the brief chances of coherent simplicity, his muse is still for the most part violent : mete-
oric, acrobatic, and garrulous in turns. The visionary
power, the spiritual excitement are abundant, but the
derivative young poet of these poems who is so fond
of "sporting with the tresses of the sun," who "dares my
hand to lay on the thunder in its snorting," to whom
day is "a dedicated priest," twilight "a violet-cassocked
acolyte," the sun a roaring lion—this young poet is
often a trial. He seems to have steeped the uncouth and
obsolete side of the English language in a Vesuvius,
and as it cools he hurls the words like stones or threshed
grain on his pages. His imagination with its vast, eccentric wings is stunning, fantastic, terrible, and might-
ily artificial in turns. Yet we must gratefully acknow-
ledge his casual approaches towards sweetness. Some
day the gods may train and simplify his power for a
mere earthly use ; he has made passes at the sun, moon,
and stars, and danced about them to a wild chorus long
enough.

But Mr. Thompson is not intellectually his own master altogether. Is he not of the fold of Mrs. Meynell?
And to the minds of all in that fold an intellectual divinity doth hedge Mrs. Meynell. She can do no literary
or critical wrong. Young men and young women of her
sphere speak about her in much the same way as loyal

Britons spoke of the Queen in the height of the Jubilee period. They move in an all-golden afternoon of poetry, an afternoon whose atmosphere and "colour of life" are altogether reflective of the mind and outlook of the gifted authoress of "Preludes." They have re-arranged the ethics of old chivalry to suit modern conditions, and they are all valiant pen-folk ready and eager to do the behests and spread the law of Her who is supreme arbitress on any question of English poetry. They were in no wise shaken in their deference even by her "Flower of the Mind" anthology and the transcending positiveness with which she set herself to "gather nothing that does not over-pass a certain boundary-line of genius," declaring in effect : Know all men by these presents the popular English poetry of the eighteenth century is to all intents and purposes wiped out. Be it therefore enacted by and with the consent of Mr. Francis Thompson, the *Academy* staff, and all others within the Meynell Privy Council assembled that with slight exceptions the period from Dryden to Burns is null and void, and of no further interest to the devotees of English poetry. One gets really anxious as to what period Mrs. Meynell and her school may next decide on and mark out for demolition.

Returning to our direct track we meet Mr. Henley with his vehement fervour ; and amongst others between us and the undistinguished mass there is the classic-cum-Celtic Dr. Todhunter, who should be remembered for *Helena in Troas* and *The Banshee and other Poems*, and the voluminous but not uniform Professor

Savage Armstrong. Mrs. Shorter's humanised spells and mystical pathos are a more recent but a clear gain. Mr. Binyon's softer felicities appeal to others, but seem unduly well regarded.

But still, very little of all this is vital enough to go down the centuries, little of it is strong enough to serve its time, to change or guide any current of contemporary thought and life. Some of it is drab-made and meanly formed, more of it skilful imitation; the best and sweetest of it little better than pleasance-places between the Peaks of Song. No; it is not a sign of the Millennium.

A WORD WITH THE EVENING
PAPERS

Mr. Birrell's disappointment is with the morning papers; mine is with those of the evening. There are many reasons for our serious if not our pretentious attitude towards life and things, towards South Africa, Westminster, the North Pole, and the Monroe Doctrine in our train and tram interludes between breakfast and business. We consciously or unconsciously look to our great dailies to sustain us in our sense that we own the earth, and that wisdom will die with us; and to do them justice, we seldom look in vain. By the evening and our return all the old frets and disillusions have beat the air and trounced the earth, twisted our nerves, and glowered at us through our city fogs. Then, oh then, accursed be the papers that take things seriously. A little fun at such hours is the saving salt of life. Apart from all this, a hundred comedies, a hundred eccentricities and amusing flashes of character have leaped to life amid the squalid damnation of the police-courts. Half Shakespeare's plays have been played unconsciously in dock and witness box; yet our journals that should pulse and scintillate with feeling, frolic, and comedy, are content to leave the whole with the recital of what "sub-constable XYZ deposed" as to the behaviour and record of "the prisoner," and the "blank shillings" or "blank days" which the "learned magistrate" imposed upon the offender. In paltry detail, in shipshod verbiage, in awkward and unrevealing description our daily tragedies and humours are dulled and deadened; London is belied, daubed where she should be painted, her history left unwritten; the heavy trail of the police-court reporter lying ugly and prone on material meet for artist and poet. Cow's amble and shuffle through brooks of gleaming life where the nymphs and graces should disport themselves.

I have by me a few random stories from the daily revelations of London life in the police and the County Courts; and I put it seriously to our evening papers whether it is not high time that they should revolutionize their method of representing these things. Gentlemen of the press, this is the artist's province; you might effect a profound difference in London's mind and thought, you might create a new note in literature by seeing that the treatment accorded to it is proper. You might—but let me try in my own way to illustrate the new order in your news columns.

I find first of all a detailed and rather ineffective story, the pith of which is that William —, Stockbroker, made a slight mistake on his way home to South Norwood. He was found lying in the mud at Sufferance Wharf, Lambeth, when the tide was out. He explained that he thought it was a railway station, and he was

waiting for the next train. At the local court the fine
was 20s. Now I submit that the following is the better
way to put William's tragedy :

In the inns on the highway and by-way
    Full flagons he drained at a draught,
"My life-path will ne'er be a dry way,"
    Said William, and loudly he laughed.
And the deeds that he did in his drinking
    Were dire, but they utterly dwarf
'Mid the things that befell him on sinking
    In Sufferance Wharf.

He came and he mused on the bank low;
    The tide had gone far to the sea—
He came, and he saw, and he sank low:
    "O soft bed of roses!" said he.
"Each rose of the rose-dreaming poet
    'Mid these was a poor, paltry bud—
O apex of bliss, now I know it"—
    And he rolled in the mud.

Then he dreamed that he sat in a station
    Whose portals of pure gold were wrought.
He rose, and in sweet agitation
    The next train to Norwood he sought.
Dream-porters, dream-clerks were around him,
    But never a word they would speak—
Said the mud-ridden William, "Confound them!
    'Tis like their d— cheek."

But I shorten the song of his sorrow—
    The watchman who roped him to land,
The p'liceman, the fine on the morrow,
    Are items you'll all understand.
Now though sober as judge is—in story—
    And pledged to be steady and good,
Ah! he misses the glamour and glory
    Of that hour in the mud.

Robert Helmsley claimed damages at the Bow County Court for injuries sustained in a raid made upon him by one of Robert Frost's cows as he crossed the peaceful fields of Leytonstone. He drew an ominous picture of this cow with her strange and stern mien. The defence was that Mr. Helmsley's fears had run away with him, and that in his riot of apprehension he fell into the adjacent ditch while the cow looked stolidly on, or wonderingly like the well-fed cow in the poet Laureate's garden. Judgment for the defendant.

O her looks were as grim as grim could be,
　　And her eyes were sad and stern,
And a gleam of the cow-world's gaiety
　　She never seemed to learn.
From all other cows that Bob Frost kept
　　In the fields of Leytonstone,
She stood apart as the long years crept—
　　As the weird cow-sphinx she was known!

And the seers that came and the seers that went
　　Were appalled at her Gorgon-eyes.
"She looks on man with a fell intent—
　　Keep far all ye who are wise!"
And a legend grew with the creeping years
　　That the cow was a demon dire,
That at night she raced all around the spheres
　　Upon feet of Inferno fire!

And the dreamy eve that Bob Helmsley came
　　She looked so hard at *him*
That into the ditch fell his quivering frame,
　　And the sight of his eyes grew dim.
And he dreamed that the cow came with demon horn
　　And lifted him high in air
Till he touched the moon and the stars of morn!—
　　He awoke— cow and ditch were there!

And he went to the County Court of Bow
  Where the sly judge laughed at his moan,
And said: "Those stories are all so-so
  Of that cow of Leytonstone."
Bob Helmsley groaned as he went away
  Full many a weary groan,
And he cursed, and he'll curse to his dying day
  That cow of Leytonstone!

The next is a record of the days when The Woman Who Would and The Woman Who Wouldn't were agitating London. The heat wave also was intolerable in the physical world. A young man appeared before the Thames Court magistrate, and pleaded that his young wife had refused to live with him. Since the wedding, seven weeks previously, she had locked herself in her room when he was "about," till that morning —when she disappeared altogether. Failing Victoria Cross, the author of "Paula," "The Woman Who Didn't," and such hare-brained heroines, the average editor might rest satisfied, perhaps,with this treatment of the situation :

A fair and dainty youth was he, yet grief was on his
    brow.
He moaned "Great Thames Court magistrate, despair's
    my portion now.
Romance is dead and joy is lost, and all great London
    seems
A blacker haunt than Dante saw in his infernal dreams."
"Hush," cried the Thames Court magistrate, "be brave
    and face the worst.
The heat will surely end ere long, and snow-storms o'er
    us burst."
Then frenzied was the young man's laugh. "The heat,
    forsooth," said he.
"I fear it not, however hot, 'tis love that tortures me.

"I won for wife a bonny lass. But seven weeks ago
Did she a bride stand by my side in spotless robes of
    snow.
All nature sang our wedding song in myriad melodies:
I heard it in the traffic's roar, and in the murmuring
    breeze.

"But ghostly was the change that came as soon as night
    loomed down:
My love grew darker than the dark, her fair face all
    a-frown.
She jeered at love, at me she sneered, then left me
    haughtily,
And sweeping to her room above, she swiftly turned
    the key.

"And since that hour at me and man she's never ceased
    to rail.
And now she's gone and won't return; and that's my
    sorry tale."

"She's New as any Bodley Belle," the magnate cried in
    awe,
And then he told the weeping youth that no redress he
    saw;
For all these wild-souled Decadents are far beyond the
    law.

At Shoreditch County Court William Bloggs sued
Emma Black, a widow, for compensation for evening
jobs at gardening. Emma pathetically contended how
she understood he was working all the time out of pure
friendship, on which understanding she had feasted him
and his wife with·tea, shrimps and other dainties. His
action was the sorest tragedy of her life. In fact Pathos

came with wan, woe-wasted eyes through her story of friendship overshadowed and man's duplicity and self-ishness. She had to pay all the same.

Said Emma Black to William Bloggs, "How could you
    ask a fee
For all that pretty gardening you did of late for me?
You came as friend, you worked as friend, with heart
    and right good will
And ne'er I thought, dear heart, you'd send that wicked
    little bill.

"You know you brought your wife each day. I gave you
    tea and jam;
I gave you shrimps and muffins, too; for generous I am.
With feast and toil each dulcet eve passed gloriously
    away.
Then, William Bloggs, I'd ne'er believe I'd see this bill-
    black day."

'Twas at the Shoreditch County Court her sobbing tale
    was told,
And though she was a widow lone the judge's heart
    was cold.
For all her teas and all her tears, she *must* pay William
    Bloggs.
O world! these unromantic years, You're going to the
    dogs!

Rose Howe, a fair young laundress of Kennington, set a fire alarm a-going at night for the sake of a "lark." Her "lark" cost her 40s. next day at Lambeth. Surely her airy abandon, her devotion to the songful impulse

within her, deserve a laureate. She was really realis-
ing herself, as Ibsen would say:

O sing the hour, the brooding hour, when Kennington
            was dark;
And Rosie Howe, the laundress fair, went out upon a
            "lark."

"Of all the birds," said Rosie Howe, "that charm the
            East or West,
My little 'lark' that sings at night is brightest still and
            best.
And sweetly in my airy heart it's made its little nest."

And then she pulled the fire alarm, and weird the deep
            bell rang.
"Oh! did you hear my little 'lark'? How very sweet it
            sang?"

"I heard it," said the constable, slow on his midnight beat.
"I have no doubt the magistrate will think it very sweet."

And Mr. Denman said the fine would forty shillings be.
And Rosie's little "lark" no more will thrill in melodee.

Lizzie Butler was uproarious at Christmas-tide,
and made a sad picture in the West London dock. She
pleaded the kindly, over-powering effects of the season.
A whole drama is here—too subtle for the reporter's
paragraph:

    "O, Lizzie Butler, of Porten road,
    Your eyes are blacker than Nature's black.
    And your face, that in old days with roses glowed.
    Is drawn and wintry, alack! alack!

"And the p'liceman tells me," said Mr. Lane,
While all ears were strained in West London Court,
"That drink has muddled your once bright brain,
That you've awful notions of play and sport.

"That you startled Hammersmith— peaceful place!—
When the night was late and the stars were deep.
That—O, Lizzie, blush for the dire disgrace—
You broke that poor constable's midnight sleep."

Then Lizzie spake: "I had cause, sweet cause.
My heart was stirred with a strange, sweet pain.
For my oldest sweetheart was Santa Claus,
And I drank for joy that he comes again."

"O, Go! Go! Go!" said the magistrate,
"We punish not love in this court of ours;
'Tis wilful, wayward, but always great—
The sweetest power of all Nature's powers."

The next story is of the tragic ending of girlhood's
trust: and man is not the deceiver this time:

'Twas in a model dwelling
    In blissful Felix-street,
Maud Chidgey with Ciss Druey dwelt
    And all their days were sweet.
They told each other tenderly,
    While each to each was true,
They'd ask no other love in life,
    Whatever swains might woo.

Maud Chidgey kissed Ciss Druey's lips,
    And said, "You little dear,
You're more to me than any swain
    In all earth's sordid sphere."

137

Ciss Druey dreamed the live-long night,
  Of Maud the fond and true
And thought if Maud e'er left her sight,
  Now much she'd pine and rue.

Yet Maud is gone, and Cissy's eyes
  Show not a tear to-day.
The prison gates have on her closed,
  Yet Cissy's heart is gay.
And oft she cries: "Old Maud, you were
  The horridest of things,
To say you loved me, then to steal
  My three bright, lovely rings!"

Our next item is a foreign one, but of course our method is not for London only. This tale is of a truth stranger than fiction—in the Punjab. A one-eyed, bald-headed ancient loved and won (he thought) a bonny lass of Ferozepore. All was ready ; the marriage procession started, but the fear overshadowed the processionists that at the last moment the bride's parents (who had not yet seen him) would refuse their consent to her union with so unprepossessing a bridegoom. The one-eyed man bethought him of a plan. He persuaded a comely barber's boy to don his gala clothes, and personate the happy man of the occasion.

This was done, the marriage passed happily over, the party returned home, the ancient thanked the youth for his services, and smilingly turned to bear away his loved one. But the youthful barber smiled in return, and absolutely refused to part with the maiden. All the entreaties of the ancient were in vain. A suit for the recovery of the bride was filed against the youth. He laughed, having a shrewd suspicion that all the facts (including the fair one herself) were in his favour.

THE ANCIENT'S PLAINT

Though I've but one eye in my pate uncouth,
  I still can plainly see
'Twas a paltry trick, O Punjab youth,
  The trick you've tried on me.

'Twas a mean, mean trick, O Punjab lad,
On a poor bald man to play— ·
To keep the bride that he all but had
  To cheer life's waning day.

O sweet she smiled in the morning mild
  'Neath the bonny Indian sky,
As I passed to church, with no thought of the lurch
  I'd be left in by-and-bye.

I thought it hard on the marriage morn
  She should stand by a fright like me,
"So lad of grace, you can take my place
  For the nonce," I said, "He! he!"

"And when all is o'er to Ferozepore
  She'll come to my home and me,
And I'll prove so kind she'll never mind
  How bald my sconce may be."

But the knot once tied, with you by her side,
  You snapped your fingers all,
And with smile and scoff you bore her off,
  And left me in sorrow's thrall.

And I curse all day while serene and gay
  Your life with the lass goes by;
The blazing fire of my natural ire
  Is wasting my other eye.

In Cupid's court but scoff and sport
    I've proved for the gods and thee;
But a suit at law—O fudge! pshaw!
    My bride is lost for me.

I need not pursue the illustration of this method of interpreting the home and foreign tidings of the day. Thus briefly and plainly set forward I trust that it speaks for itself.

MAINLY FOR Mr. BIRRELL

I tell this story to prove to Mr. Birrell that newspa-
pers are even worse than he thought them. Journalists
made a sad set on him because in the "quiet season," or
thereabouts, in the year of grace '97, he made graceful fun of their pretensions. Yet cross-grained indeed
must be the man who grows nasty when Mr. Birrell
birrelleth. That the thing is possible at all shows how
badly out of order are our fin-du-siècle nerves : what
miserable stuff has returned with some of our receding
brain-waves.

Perhaps the man who invented the not unhappy
term "Birrelling" has helped to do some wrong to the
modest author of "Obiter Dicta." "Birrelling" suggests
lightness and graceful irresponsibility, pleasant thin-
ness, charming but ephemeral tinklings. It is in that
acceptation, which will be found a not uncommon one,
an injustice to Mr. Birrell. In one of his own phrases,
his thoughts and essays are indeed "light and graceful,
but it would be unjust to call them slender." A sense of
widening horizons he brings. "Something of the cool-

ing of falling water, something of the music of rustling trees," many pretty keys of playfulness, a sane, shrewd, worldly-wise, yet reverential outlook ; the capacity to see the inherent manliness and beauty and hope of things, yet the spirit to see and delightfully expose the comedy or crudeness of their sometime exteriors—all these he shows. A cultured man, a book-lover, a book-connoisseur, his garb has not a speck of library dust, his eyes none of the blurred, limited vision of the book-worm. He has the child's interest in the tender, weak, and lowly things abroad in nature, the man's manly interest in the panorama of the hills and fields, the philosopher's and Christian's interest in the broad, ever-varying, intense, and sometimes terrible ocean of human progress. He has grappled with big and solemn problems, but in his setting forth of his conclusions his charm and instinctive gentleness seldom desert him, while his young and refreshing playfulness often peeps in. The best of democrats, because cultured, unselfish, and healthy, he is at home with the man of the world, the theologian, and the scholar, though to be sure, in some of his moods and modes he no more than nibbles at his subject, if I may be pardoned the phrase. But this is carrying us too far from the evening papers and Radford's tragedy.

It seemed a happy hour in the life of Radford. Yet everyone else in the dingy editorial rooms of the *Gloaming* was sorry—sorry that after twenty years' service Radford was going. Radford indeed, had been "going" for years, but circumstances had turned up to prevent the great severance. But now the time had come when he fully believed he could devote his life to romance and the deferred high purpose of two decades.

Radford's had been a curious history. Twenty years before, he had come up, a blithe youth of eighteen, from a corner of East Anglia, eager-hearted, and confident that he would win a name as a novelist. He had written the first chapter of "The Strange Adventures of Miss Kilkins," and before the end of the first volume there were to be amazing developments. But while writing Radford must live, and he blessed the chance that threw in his way at the outset a post as reporter on the *Gloaming.* Was not journalism the kindred field to literature, if not literature itself? From his reporting duties to his study and his beloved MS. would be just a pleasant transition. He would be an English Gautier. Yes, he had begun well.

In the long years Radford had—well, disappointments. His stories of murders, fires, inquests, burglaries, revelations at the Old Bailey, were not the best aids to the style he desired. A poignant Hardy (of the earlier manner) set amid the flavour of primroses, someone had called a little MS. he brought to London at the outset. Soon it would have seemed a ghastly jest. And then he was always in a hurry. Hurry! Why, a lost spirit doomed to a perpetual rush from one quarter of the globe to another were not less certain of peace than he. To "write up" a club raid in Aldgate, a street fight in Chelsea, to hurry away to Notting Hill to secure a better story of the afternoon murder and suicide than the rival paper might compass—these were ordinary items of the everyday struggle. When he turned home to his Peckham lodgings he reviewed the situation with pitiful feelings. Every night he reverently took down his MS. of the first chapter of "Miss Kilkins," but in such a state of fatigue that he could not add a sentence that satisfied him.

He would have thrown up the work but for that early romance that dazzled him, and hold him ever after—his love for Hettie Ferguson. The prospect of married life made him timorous. He could not run risks; he wanted a certainty for Hettie's sake.

Queer developments ensued for Radford. His career as a novelist was still his golden ideal; but only an ideal as year succeeded year. He had still to toil for a competence—for the end when he could prudently marry Hettie. Intolerably long it was in coming.

Meanwhile he often outdid his rivals; achieved "scoops," in reporting parlance, every week of the year. Give him a hint that anything particular was happening, and he was aflame till he had got to the heart of it. He made a big fortune for the *Gloaming*, and gradually a little one for himself.

So, at last, he saw his way to marrying Hettie, to retiring from the *Gloaming*, to devoting himself to that long deferred work of fiction. And now, as he said "good-bye," he could hardly realise that his wedding was three days hence, that his literary career would begin as the honeymoon ended. Radford was ungovernably happy. In leisure moments he glowed over the first MS. of "Miss Kilkins." In the solemn nights he kissed it reverently.

Radford and his pretty but somewhat sad-faced wife were standing on the evening of their wedding-day on the platform of the suburban station whence they would depart for the south and the honeymoon. Somehow they seemed overpensive for newly-wedded folk, and Radford was plainly unrestful.

Suddenly, as the train approached, there was a wild cry in one of the streets below. A heavy fall, and a woman's voice shrieked "Murder!" Mrs. Radford shuddered. But now the train was alongside the platform. "We will go in here, dear," she said.

But, lo! Radford was not at her side. He must have been pushed apart, she thought, in the struggle of the crowd. But now nearly everyone had either taken seats or turned to the exit-door, yet Radford was nowhere to be seen. Puzzled, she ran from carriage to carriage. There was still no trace of him! The train steamed out of the station. Mrs. Radford was left alone.....

Radford came back with an excited look on his face. "Quite a scoop," he cried. "When I heard the woman's cry I knew there was a story in it. I got it all from the landlady while the police were seeing to Mrs. Hudson. The villain has cut his own throat. Jealousy was the cause of the crime. I've wired it all to the *Gloaming.* What! you've been crying? Good Heavens! is the train gone? Well, well, we must go to the Hotel— until to-morrow." . . .

Radford and his wife got separated at Blackfriars.

A fire was raging on the Surrey side, and crowds were hurrying across the bridge. Instinctively Radford ran. Then he cursed his thoughtlessness, for he could not find trace or tidings of his wife. The quest lasted for hours. At last he hurried to the Hotel—Mrs. Radford was standing patiently, but wearily, near the door in the chilly night.

*

* *

The honeymoon had been over some months, as Radford, pallid and fretful, hurried one day to his old friend, Gilgan, the publisher.

"Gilgan," said he, in a ghostly tone, "I'm a cursed man. The one dream of my life has been a quiet time when I could write the novel that I planned twenty years ago. But the quiet kills me. I can't endure it. I can't write. I've grown old in reporting fever, and there's no rest for me. I've tried to mend matters by putting a terrible fire in the second chapter, a murder in the third, an abduction in the fourth, an Old Bailey trial in the fifth, a Newgate execution in the sixth. But it won't do, for it isn't art. Now, perhaps, I could arrange matters with you. You agree to publish it—fair terms, you know—I to have the MS. ready by an early date. Being tied down to the thing, I must get through it. Otherwise I can't; and I'll go to mad. Yes, Gilgan, I'll go mad."

He told Gilgan the plot, and described the characters.

146

"Would never do," said Gilgan. "School and style of twenty years ago. No money in it now. Nobody would review it or read it. Mr. Crockett might just as well try to write like Mrs. Radcliffe."

Radford groaned. "Gilgan, I'll go mad," he cried.

"Never despair!" said Gilgan. "Write me a little novel of this character"—he entered into a long explanation—"bring in a Scotch character or two. Your wife is Scotch, and you can easily manage it. She can translate your plain English into Kailyard as you go along. That's what pays best nowadays, unless you can manage a Big Drink Story." •

The would-be author was dubious.

A month later Radford called again. He was like a spectre.

"The task is hopeless," he cried. "I can write of nothing but fires, murders, and inquests. My life is ruined."

.... That self-same night, as a wild storm raged over South London, Radford woke up from a troubled sleep. As he rubbed his eyes, an appalling lightning-flash seemed to glow in the very street. "What a fire!" he cried, as he dashed to the window and opened it. "I'm first on the scene again. First, by Jove, first!"

The next moment he had crashed to the pavement. The following day he died.

A sad theme, and it is hardly meet to suggest sadness in connection with the author for whom I have written it. So in the hope of winning the reader to a lighter humour I transcribe the particulars here of a "Dream of Mr. Birrell," the first of a series to be named "Authors I Have not Seen." At the outset I dealt with his literary personality: this is the vision of his personal significance.

Here, then is the Dream's burden:

Mr. Birrell's individuality is timidly, yet definitely, proclaimed in his clothes. They are "cut saucy," to use an East-end phrase. They are smart, they suggest thoughts of something dapper, and they are a little too short for him. Yet somehow even the *Tailor and Cutter* could not call them inartistic. They are neither new nor old; they are like a mellow volume whose age one never thinks of inquiring into. They may not have been carefully planned, but if not, then they are a happy accident. The fact remains that though they suit him they are still a little too short for him. Hence when he stands on a platform—he is always metaphorically standing on a platform—one gets the impression that he is an angel without his wings.

It does not mean that he has lost his wings, but, getting separated from his company of fellow-angels, he has taken them off, put them under his waistcoat, and has resolved, till he gets caught, and re-robed and re-winged, to make a little flippant sport for mortals. From time to time as he utters his *mots* he glances sideways and a little timidly over his shoulders, fearing the arrival of his captors. Sometimes he feels that at last they *are* close at hand, and he grows angelically serious, says deep things with his eyes on the ground, as if in all innocence and solemnity he were cultivating a mission to set mortals in the way they should go. In any case he knows his captors must shortly find him, so he hurries through his remarks. So many pert things come into mind that they crush one another, and it is difficult to get them out. He stammers, and it would seem that along with uttering dainty flippancies he is chewing small toothsome nuts to make him feel at home and comfortable.

He affects manners of playful maidenhood, and would like to feel shy and blush, but he cannot manage it. He tries again, but it's no use, and this upsets him slightly. By this time he has realised that the human outlook is vastly different from his, and that a number of things which are natural to him somewhat puzzle, perplex, or even irritate his audience. The temptation to rile them grows. He riles them a little more. He sees a dozen sides, of which they know nothing, to earthly questions, and he turns these round with a Puck-like alertness. All the time he is making dry little smiles dance in the corners of his eyes.

He soon gets tired of it all, and simmers slow and looks meek. He works in a witty thing about the decadence of the cabbage-plant, the æsthetic side of the mangold-wurtzel, or the influence of mustard on the genius of Robert Browning. He tries lightest persiflage and homely commonplace, yet auditors don't understand him, and he wonders why they take the one and the other so gratefully and unsuspiciously from Mr. Austin Dobson and Mr. George R. Sims.

Then he remembers his angelic origin and pardons them.

Still they have put him rather in a cranky mood, and he is roused to do a queer thing. He goes off and proffers a contribution to the *Speaker*, and the irony of the thing is that Sir Wemyss Reid, who has inveighed so seriously against the "bumptious snippet," accepts it in good faith. Yet—knowing Sir Wemyss's weakness—Mr. Birrell has deliberately palmed off a lot of "bumptious snippets" in his contribution. Indeed, all his neatest things, mixed up in articles long or short, are "bumptious snippets." But he has disguised them so daintily that Sir Wemyss and half the world never find out the trick. And he, who is a wag, shakes the wings inside his waistcoat and laughs.

A COMING CRISIS

WHY THE EARTH STOOD STILL

The Sun surveyed his solar realm in an angry mood one morning towards the close of the summer of 19—. The Moon had been on duty the previous night, and now looked down in a sober, melancholy, and utterly pessimistic mood on the drab-coloured earth. The Sun called loudly three or four times to her Moonship, but she took no notice.

"Helloa!" exclaimed the Sun, this time fairly bellowing across the ethereal expanse. His voice was like the first peal of a morning thunderstorm. The Moon barely raised her eyebrows. A budding astronomer in the suburbs, fortunately the only one of his kind awake, prepared a long letter on the phenomenon for his favourite morning paper.

Again the Sun spoke, and this time the Moon answered. The ensuing dialogue may be described as a talk in thunder.

"What is the matter with that earth of yours?" shouted the Sun. "I haven't had time to attend closely

151

to its internal affairs of late. Uranus has tried to get off the track, and has kept me busy breaking him in. And the new planet beyond Neptune is a mad-headed youngster entirely, and comet tactics are more in his line. Besides, the attempt to close half the public-houses in Jupiter has almost caused a revolution there. So my hands have been pretty full."

"Well, you should have tried coercion," said the Moon. "As for the earth, I don't know what to make of it. Time was when I had some influence over it."

"The poets used to be very fond of you," said the Sun slyly.

"Ay," said the Moon, somewhat sorrowfully. "They were a little extravagant in their praises from time to time, but they were sincere. Now they don't bother about me. They lilt to the New Woman and the other absurdities that have come up like mushrooms in the British Isles."

"To tell the truth," said the Sun, "I don't know very much about the progress of things in that little planet at all. It has grown stupid within the last century or so. I only know that it seems very difficult to turn it on its axis of late. Some days it almost stands stock still, and a block in the solar traffic has seemed imminent."

"I've noticed it myself," said the Moon. "Maybe the axis is getting rusty."

"Not a bit of it," replied the Sun, "'tisn't quite a hundred years since I had a new one put in. Some ter-ribly heavy bodies must have fallen on the planet lately."

This was only the first of many anxious colloquies

held between the Sun and Moon in after days. Meanwhile the earth's affairs were getting more and more unmanageable. Once or twice it seemed as if there were absolutely no chance of turning it on its axis within the regulaton time. It stood a dull, inert mass in space, The stars that knew its old fair mien and its merry minstrelsy were sad upon their aerial thrones. It was suggested to the Sun that he should move it altogether out of the solar system, and place it in the Home for Disabled Planets.

His spirit messengers brought him reports one morning on reading which he promptly made up his mind. "How stupid of us all not to have solved the mystery before," said he.

It came to pass that on a certain afternoon London was quite deserted. Londoners, in their pre-occupied state, never paused to think how it had all been managed, but managed it was. The whole inhabitants of the city had gathered to the Crystal Palace grounds and the neighbourhood. Strange performances had been announced by strange visitors to the city, but the fact that a billiard handicap, a social purity discussion, a horse-race, a dog-fight, a meeting of the Vagabonds' Club, and a New Woman's Congress were coming off in the vicinity would have practically sufficed to clear the city.

As evening advanced dread noises were heard over the heart of the city, clouds gathered, winds rose, and there seemed imminent a combination of the twin terrors of a solar eclipse and a tornado. Furies howled in the air, and the faces of the distant Londoners blanched with terror. The voices of doom seemed in the world.

A troop of spirits congregated near Charing Cross. The scene was surpassingly weird. They paused for awhile.

" 'Tis time the collectors were here," said the chief spirit.

"Ah, but the loads they have to bring are heavy," said another.

As the scene grew darker a number of other spirits trooped in, heavily laden with sundry articles whose heaviness crushed and pained them, spirits though they were. The chief spirit looked on sadly as the various loads were dropped before him. "Unfortunate land! Deluded people," he muttered. At length the whole articles were unloaded, and a startling pile they made. The chief spirit glanced down the list:—

50,000 copies Hall Caine's Christian (1st Edition).
20,000   „   „   „   „   (2nd Edition).
The Works of Marie Corelli.
"The Beauties of Marie Corelli." (Edited by Annie Mackay).
The Logs rolled by Le Gallienne & Co.
1 Poet Laureate.
1,000,000,000,000 volumes of the New Humour.
The Fabian Essays.
The international pronouncements of Mr. Jerome K. Jerome.
The Literature of the Kailyard.
1 copy New Irish Library.
100,000 "Precipitated" Mahatma letters lent by Mrs. Besant.
200 spooks by Mr. Stead.
The Independent Theatre.

Mr. Clement Scott's articles in the *Daily Telegraph*.
The Expresses on the Chatham & Dover Railway.
The Influence of Madame Blavatsky.
Mr. Lane's Decadents.
The *Bookman's* "New Writers."
Crumbs from a Prince's serviette. Collected by Mrs. B-ll-c L-wnd-l-c.

"Brother spirits," said the chief, "what a sad proof have we here of human degeneracy! No wonder the poor encumbered planet could not move. We have been through the whole solar system, and heavier, more deadening material, we have never met. You're sure there are no more of these things abroad?"

"Not another," was the answer.

"Under the 'logs'," said one spirit, "we met a sad sight. The bodies of a dozen log-rollers were crushed to pieces. It was worse than the old story of the stone of Sisyphus. The gods, I suppose, got sickened at last, and crushed the poor fellows under the last load of logs they had devised. I am rather sorry for Richard Le Gallienne, but as for others—"

"Let us burn these sad things to ashes," broke in the chief spirit.

It was easier said than done. They tried all sorts of fiery contrivances, but the articles would not ignite. Dull smoke puffed up in clouds, fitful little gleams flashed out, but still in a dreary, lightless mass stood the medley.

"Ah!" cried the chief spirit suddenly, "fetch one of Robert Buchanan's old controversies in the *Chronicle* or *Telegraph*. They're the most heated and heating things I know of."

Soon the scene was weirder. The pile was in a blaze. The spirit of each article leaped to blazing life in the conflagration and as the last mass turned to ashes went howling away to distant lands of night and doom. The earth once more was able to revolve peacefully and easily on her axis. The horrified Londoners came up from the Palace and all turned over new leaves.

SPARROW-WORSHIP IN LITERATURE

(A COMING BOOM)

"Well, I'm damned!" twittered the old Temple sparrow.

"Sir!" said his better half, indignantly, rousing herself from a peculiarly moody mood, glancing first at her mate, and then shrugging her shoulders as her attention was attracted to the drip of the rain underneath.

"Pardon me, my dear," he said. "I was stupidly unconscious of your presence for a moment; I heard something to-day of a revival of an old grievance of ours—a silly popular display of interest in our neighbours, the Temple pigeons. The question you know crops up from time to time, when the pigeons are threatened with extermination by the Temple authorities. The public awake to the significance and historic associations of the pigeons and write letters to the *Daily Telegraph*. It has happened more than once in our own day. I am not so young as I once was—nay, I am no longer young, save in your affections and in your mind's eye, my queen—but I cannot remember the great *B. P.* getting excited over anything so trivial, I don't even except Miss Corelli's portrait.

"Strange, my ownest own," said his better half, "I was pondering on the same topic. 'Tis high time that the boom were on again. But you seem to treat it rather jauntily."

"And by all the wigs and gowns, why should you be wounded over it, my treasure? Don't you see its side-splitting points, my rose-lovely twitterer."

"But consider," she said, while her eyes softened at his flattery, "consider the nice things that have been said in past years, and will be said again of these inane and brainless pigeons—the foolish, milk-and-water creatures who don't know their own minds an hour, who are as chicken-hearted as anything in London, and whose gait and general deportment are subjects of standing worry and disgust to the eyes of any species of femininity. And——"

"But, my own——"

"Pardon me, my love, I am excited, and I must say my say. Not satisfied with praising and pleading for these mopish and perfectly horrid pigeons, the people will go out of their way to ridicule us—us, my dear! They call us noisy vagabonds, and refer with withering scorn to some of our free-and-easy Bohemian habits."

Her mate chuckled.

"Don't trouble yourself, my sensitive pet," he said. "People who use the language you describe are only a few hare-brained idealists and romanticists. And I, who have read the signs of the times, have often told you that the reign of such folk is over. The world, you know, is veering more and more to the realistic. And in the life, ways, and principles (if I may so call them) of the sparrow, there is much, very much, my sweet, that must appeal to the realist."

"I am afraid you are a mere airy theorist," said his better half, in an incredulous tone.

"Ah, you are not convinced, my charming one. You feminines fix your eyes so insistently on small points that you entirely lose the sense of great issues. But let me leave the big issues and tendencies and come to individual and isolated things that you can readily understand. In our own day haven't we witnessed the white-washing of every historical blackguard and blockhead that you can think of? Nowadays the historian considers himself blessed if he can find a still unwhitewashed or unhonoured historical blackguard or nonentity. Why, I have heard that somebody has written a book in praise of Satan Montgomery—you know your Macaulay, of course. Do you imagine that in an age of such tendencies, the sparrow, with all his bold, breezy, brazen, and racy characteristics, will be left long without his enthusiastic admirers and interpreters? My dear, the day of sparrow-worship is coming. The mere pigeon will be simply laughed at."

"That certainly is a promising view," the better half said, somewhat hopefully.

"To be sure it is. We sparrows are bluff and British, when all is said and done. We smack of the rude seas.

We have the Beerbohm note, without perhaps the Beerbohm polish. We twitter what we think. As a new Tennyson might say :—

> It was our ancient privilege, my birds,
> To fling whate'er we felt unfearing into twitters.

So much for our noise. As to other habits of ours, such tactics have been immortalised for all time by that fellow Wordsworth, who talks of the good old rule, the simple plan.

> That they may take who have the power,
> And they may keep who can.

Do you follow me, my fons et origo of love?"

"I wish you wouldn't talk that way," she said, very crossly. "You know, you wild fellow, that I wasn't your first love."

After this it took a good deal of coaxing and compliments to bring her to her usual self. Then they turned to the pigeon-sparrow question again. Finally, they adjourned the discussion, after heartily congratulating themselves that one sad joke formerly put upon the pigeon world had not been offered to them. No one had suggested—as the *Daily Graphic* had once on a time in connection with the pigeons—that Norman Gale should appeal to public sympathy with a poem in their behalf!

"For which relief much thanks," they twittered.

THE LOVER OF MISS LUCIFER
LEXICON

Dashem was brilliant, whimsical, and wayward.
Dashem was a figure, a personality in the suburbs.
Dashem had an independent income, and that in the
eyes of suburban mammas covered a multitude of eccentricities and mental vagaries.

Dashem overflowed with ideas. He knew he had a
mission in the world, but, somehow, it kept in the vague
region of intangible things, and the would-be missionary
was unhappy. He never could endure the idea of think-
ing or working upon any line that any human being—
though great as Moses or Shakespeare (I beg Mr.
Shaw's pardon)—had tried before him. He admitted
that after all the ages during which our planet-folk have
been making experiments it would be no easy matter
to strike upon an unmistakably new line. Aubrey
Beardsley, Sherlock Holmes, and the lady-novelists
had brought the world to expect so much! But he was
certain that, sooner or later, he would strike upon the
Amazing Novelty. Humanity wanted an absolutely
new impulse. One day he told a select few of us that
he felt sure he was on the track of that impulse at last.

He began to see solar systems where before were the merest nebulæ. He grew strangely excited.

He told us later on, in a whisper almost awe-striking, that the idea was ripening fast. That was on the occasion of Lady Camberwell's never-to-be-forgotten "At Home," the occasion of his introduction to Miss Lucifer Lexicon, who had just startled London by her literary masterpiece, "Guesses at the Nature and Appearance of Extinct Masculinity; a study of A. D. 3995." Miss Lucifer was an early type of that perfect woman to be evolved after many painful centuries of a developing womankind trained and spoon-fed by generations of George Egertons, Sarah Grands, Dr. Arabella Kenealys, Frank Danbys, Mrs. Sarah Tooleys, and sundry such varying sorts.

Strange to relate, Dashem, who previously had been anything but a lover of feminine society, spent most of his time henceforward in the company of the fair Miss Lucifer. He assured us cynics, however, that his great idea was swiftly advancing towards fruition. He had practically completed the quaint creed that was to give permanent vitality to mankind. Miss Lucifer, he added, was an invaluable helper.

London soon learned some of Dashem's plans. The new creed was to be preached in a new evening journal which would be a very miracle as a record-breaker. The paper, type, matter, colour, arrangements were to be sensationally different from anything which London had hitherto seen. The whole would be a departure that would take not only the city's breath, but the city's fogs away. Sir George Newnes would refuse to be comforted in Lynton and there would be no more high crowing in the House of Harmsworth.

Dashem despised the idea of an ordinary editorial office. He and Miss Lucifer had invented a patent balloon, which in the summer weather would float gracefully over the city, and therein, with the peaceful clouds as their companions, they could dream, plan, write, and edit, undisturbed by the noisy trials to which common journalistic flesh was heir. Their copy would be forwarded from time to time per a minor balloon, or else an ingenious aerial telephone, to the palace in the West-end where their printing and publishing would be done amidst scenes and sights sufficient to recall Oriental magnificence. If, haply, they grew tired of the balloon, there was a golden caravansary to fall back upon. This would be driven from pretty haunt to pretty haunt in the neighbourhood of the great city, as the unique editors thought and wrote. In this way an ever-freshening impulse would be given to their fancies, an ever-brightening novelty to their outlook, in striking contrast to the stagnation and dreariness and discontent of Fleet-street.

The eve of the first issue had come. All was ready for the morrow's triumphal and epoch-making entry into the journalistic world. Dashem and Miss Lucifer were seated in the beautiful balloon, which sailed like a spirit through the dreamful ether, far, far above the prosy world. Miss Lucifer was penning one of her famous epistles, and was lost in thought. A lamp, golden and bejewelled, stood on the pretty table beside her. Dashem stood a little distance away, looking down now and then to the far dim city beneath him. For a man whose life's triumph was so near he seemed unaccountably moody. He was several times on the point of speaking, but he checked himself. At length Miss Lucifer concluded her epistle, she sealed the missive, despatched it per the patent waiting balloon at her elbow, smiled one of her superior smiles, then raised her eyebrows in surprise at the pained looks of Dashem. Her eyebrows, by the way, were expressive of a terrible strength. They seemed to tell of new femininity, anti-masculinity, stop-at-nothingness growing bolder with the days. New Women swore by them. Men trembled when they bristled.

"Why so sad, Bertie?" cried Miss Lucifer, with unmistakable impatience in her tone. "I thought you had broken for ever with these common failings and feelings of humanity."

"Alas!" said Dashem, "in this my triumph time, I blush to confess that one base weakness of Old Humanity has overpowered me. Frown not, Miss Lucifer. The gods have mocked me in this regard. I am passion's slave. Miss Lucifer I am in love. And such is the trick of fate that thou, O utterly-revolted one, art the object of my love."

New Woman though she was, Miss Lucifer could not speak for fair astonishment for the next five minutes. Dashem took advantage of the peace to plead a word in his own cause.

"Silence, weak slave!" cried Miss Lucifer, as she jumped to her feet in supreme indignation. As she leaped upward, wild with anger, her arm struck the golden lamp beside her. A noise as of thunder, leaping fire, then confusion, chaos! Balloon, Dashem, Miss Lucifer were caught in the one fierce flame that now shot a lurid, hissing, deadly light through the ether and the evening.

Only a few ashes reached the earth. That was all that was left to a waiting world of the great journalistic pioneers. Their disciples gathered the ashes up devoutly, and enshrined them in a rich shrine. Then mournfully they went out to their now lonely and desolate life-ways, sad as the New Humourists that Autumn morning when they heard of the Passing of Jerome—from *To-Day*.

THE END

[Some of the matter in "The Great Young Man," "The Flight From the Caineyard," and certain other papers, has been used on the literary page of *The Sun*, a few other pages in the *Weekly Sun*, and yet a few more in *The Senate*. Much even of this matter has been re-written, and sundry additions have been made to it, so with many of its sentiments it might not be quite fair to identify the hospitable publications in question.]